DEAD MAN'S TRAIL

Arrest the "dead man" who had suddenly come to life and was the power behind the killer gang terrorizing the border.

In this desperate, danger-packed manhunt, Texas Ranger Walt Slade, undercover ace of the Texas Rangers, found himself playing the deadliest hand Fate had ever dealt him.

DEAD MAN'S TRAIL

Bradford Scott

GUNSMOKE

This hardback edition 2006
by BBC Audiobooks Ltd
by arrangement with
Golden West Literary Agency

ISBN 10: 1 4056 8086 5
ISBN 13: 978 1 405 68086 8

British Library Cataloguing in Publication Data available.

Printed and bound in Great Britain by
Antony Rowe Ltd., Chippenham, Wiltshire

One

THE SORREL HORSE had given his all. His flanks, streaked with blood from the cruel rakings of Cullen Baker's army rowel spurs, heaved and quivered, his great chest labored. His eyes were gorged with red, as were his flaring nostrils. His breath came in sobbing gasps and his head jerked downward with each faltering stride. Cullen Baker swore viciously and again and again the spurs drove home, the vicious little rowels no larger than a dime.

Cullen Baker was a giant of a man with hot intolerant black eyes, a big nose and a mouth that was a cruel gash above his massive, jutting chin. His cheeks were furred with a stubble of black beard and his lank black hair hung down over the collar of his shirt. His face was that of an able, adroit, and utterly ruthless man. His finely formed body bespoke tremendous strength and endurance, just as his hard stare and tightly clamped lips hinted at courage and daring.

The sorrel had given his all and it wasn't enough. Still sticking relentlessly to his trail and closing the distance foot by straining foot was that black demon who, when the race for the Red River began in the early afternoon, was nearly two miles behind. Now the distant waters of the Red flashed scarlet in the dying sunlight, but the black pursuer was close! Close!

Baker's slashing quirt raised fresh welts on the sorrel's barrel, welts that oozed blood. He turned and glared over his shoulder, mouthing curses, faced to the front and raked fresh blood upon his spurs. The great black horse was nearer than when last he glanced back. Now he

5

could distinctly make out the tall form of his rider. The features of the lean hawk face were taking form and shape from the whitish blur they had been ten minutes before.

There was no blood streaking the flanks of the great black, no quirt welts oozing blood on his ribs. Ranger Walt Slade never carried one. Shadow, the horse, needed no mechanical implementing; the quiet urging of his master's voice was all that was necessary to cause him to put forth the last iota of his speed, strength and endurance.

Although he was giddy with fatigue, his glorious black coat flecked with foam and streaked with sweat, his smooth running gait reduced to little better than a shambling walk, he still forged doggedly ahead, snorting with eagerness, his eyes rolling angrily. For still in front of him, after many hours, was the golden wraith that had tested his powers to their utmost.

But Shadow still had enough left to close the gap which separated his master from the last member, the deadliest and most resourceful of the notorious Baker gang.

Shadow didn't know it, but the yellow flood of the Red River, now drawing near, was a threat to Slade's hopes of getting rid of Cullen Baker once for all. If Baker managed to get across the river he was clear of Texas soil, and ranger authority did not extend beyond the far bank. Let him reach the water and he might make it across.

Baker was now within long rifle range. Slade automatically dropped his hand toward the butt of the heavy Winchester snugged in the saddle boot beneath his left thigh, then regretfully shook his black head. A sleepless night culminating in a bitter and bloody gun battle and then the long, gruelling chase across the sun-drenched prairie were taking toll. He was blind with weariness, his nerves were raw and ragged. To attempt to bring Baker down with the Winchester would very likely only cause Shadow to falter and lose the precious distance he had strained so hard to lessen. No, the only thing was to get close enough to shoot it out with six-guns. Shadow was steadily gaining on the exhausted sorrel, but the river bank was close.

But now the sorrel was reeling and staggering. Not even the agonizing torment of spur and quirt could bring to the fore that which did not exist. He was utterly done; any minute and he would fall.

Cullen Baker also realized the fact; his mount could never make it to the river bank in time to enable him to get a head start on his pursuer after he entered the water. Still, he held on a moment longer. Then, when he was almost to the bank that fell away sheer to the deep and frothing water, he fairly hurled himself from the saddle. He made a grab for the sorrel's bridle iron, apparently intending to take shelter behind his mount, but he missed and the sorrel shambled on, head hanging. It swerved just in time to avoid going over the brink and stood with legs widespread, its sides heaving like a bellows.

Walt Slade also left his saddle. He half slid, half fell from it as Baker drew with lightning speed and opened fire. A bullet screamed through the space his body had occupied the instant before. He jerked his own guns and answered Baker shot for shot.

Slade, weaving and ducking, plunged toward the outlaw.

Back and forth through the deepening gloom spurted the red flashes, the reports a drumroll of sound. Slade whirled halfway around as a slug caught him in the left arm. The terrific shock almost knocked him off his feet. At the same instant Baker reeled back and back. On the front of his faded shirt, just above the heart, a widening dark stain appeared. Back he reeled, vainly trying to line sights with his opponent. A bullet kicked up dirt at the reeling ranger's feet. Another fanned his face. Then the gun fell from Baker's hand. Back he reeled, over the high bank. His body struck the water and instantly the current caught it and whirled it downstream. Slade, darkness coiling before his eyes, tried to follow its course. He saw a brown hand lifted in the dashing spray, then the black water rolled over it and Cullen Baker vanished from his sight.

Staggering like a drunken man Slade lurched to where Shadow stood blowing and snorting. For a moment he hung against the horse's barrel, breathing in great gasps. Grimly he fought the chill blackness that sought to swathe his brain. He could feel the blood running down his arm and dripping from his fingertips, a warm, sticky flood. If he fell unconscious he would very likely bleed to death. With shaking fingers he fumbled in his saddle pouch, dug out a roll of bandage and a jar of antiseptic ointment. With a single hard pull he ripped his left shirt sleeve free at the shoulder and let it fall to the ground. Working clumsily with one hand he managed to pad and bandage the wound. The bullet had gone through the fleshy part of his upper arm but fortunately had missed the bone.

Once the flow of blood was staunched he began to feel better. He fished tobacco and papers from his shirt pocket, awkwardly rolled a cigarette and lighted it. A couple of deep drags and he found he could stand without leaning against Shadow for support. Another moment and he stumbled to where the exhausted sorrel still stood with hanging head. He smeared the ointment on the cruel gashes left by spur and quirt. Then he led the horse up and down the bank for some minutes, gradually cooling him till his sides ceased to heave and he lifted his head. Shadow paced sedately after him, apparently none the worse for all he had undergone.

Slade found a spot where it was possible to scramble down to the water. He let the horses drink and then drank himself. The cool water refreshed him greatly. He rolled another cigarette and stood gazing at the hurrying waters of the swollen Red.

"Reckon that takes care of the Cullen Baker bunch, to the last man," he told Shadow. "And thank the good Lord, here comes the moon. Maybe we can spot someplace to cook something to eat and boil a bucket of coffee."

A few minutes later the strengthening moonlight revealed the black clump of a small grove a couple of hundred yards upstream. Slade made for it, leading the horses. The sorrel appeared well on the way to recovery. At the edge of the trees he got the rigs off the animals and turned them loose to graze.

There was plenty of dry wood in the grove and soon coffee was bubbling in a little flat bucket and bacon sizzling in a small skillet. Slade's saddle pouches also produced some flour which the heat and the bacon grease alchemized into a very tasty doughcake.

After eating the bread and meat and drinking the coffee, and feeling much revived, Slade rolled a cigarette and sat smoking with the firelight playing over his ruggedly handsome face and powerful form while he reviewed the hectic happenings of the past twenty-four hours.

Slade, with the sheriff of the county and three deputies, had surprised Cullen Baker and his bunch in their hideout. In the ensuing gun battle, three of the outlaws had died, two were captured. But Cullen Baker, the giant leader, had escaped amid a hail of bullets. Baker was splendidly mounted and the chase had lasted many hours before the great black horse had proven himself the tall sorrel's master. So, everything considered, despite the ache of his bullet-punctured arm and a deadly weariness,

Slade was fairly contented with the course of events.

Pinching out the butt of his cigarette, he stood up, towering more than six feet above the dying fire. He started to stretch his long arms above his head, then winced. The left one wasn't in very good stretching condition. He spread his blanket and arranged the saddle for a pillow. Before lying down he made sure Shadow was okay.

"In the morning we'll ride to the county seat and tell the sheriff what happened," he told the black. "Then I'll have the doctor give this scratch a once-over and we'll head back to the Post and see what next Captain Jim has lined up for us."

Shadow snorted agreement and, it is to be assumed, relayed the information to the sorrel, who didn't understand man-talk as well as he did.

A little over seven months after that grim fight on the bank of the Red River, Captain Jim McNelty, Commander of the Border Battalion of the Texas Rangers, summoned his lieutenant and ace-man to his office. He gestured Slade to a chair and rustled a sheet of paper he held in his hand.

"Here's the final dossier we made out on the Cullen Baker bunch," he remarked, passing the paper to Slade. Taking it, the ranger the Mexican peons of the Rio Grande river villages named El Halcon—The Hawk— read off a list of names with explanatory notes beside each:

Joseph McCartney—dead.
Anse Hepburn—dead.
Arthur Gardner—dead.
Willis Blaine—state prison.
Crane Wilbur—state's evidence, disposal pending.
Cullen Baker—presumed dead.

Slade raised his eyes from the document. "Well?" he asked.

Captain Jim looked contemplative. "Well," he said, "it begins to look like 'presumed' was the right word. As I recollect, Webster defines presume as 'take for granted'."

"Meaning?"

"Meaning," Captain Jim repeated, "that unless several usually reliable persons have taken to lying or are making a hell of a mistake, the presumably dead Cullen Baker is very much alive."

Slade stared at the commander. "Well," he said, "he sure looked dead when the water closed over him."

"An informant who says he knew him well swears that last month he saw Cullen Baker in Mexico, consorting with Sabida Quijano."

Slade's lips pursed in a soundless whistle. Sabida Quijano was a Mexican Border bandit who for some time had been a thorn in the flesh of peace officers on both sides of the Rio Grande. Unlike many of his ilk, he did not pose as a liberator out to start a revolution and obtain justice for the oppressed. He was a bandit leader and didn't claim to be anything else. But he had a large following south of the Border and some north of the Rio Grande. A shrewd operator, he employed the Robin Hood technique. Many a starving peon had a fistful of gold thrust into his eager palm. Also, now and then, Quijano and some of his bunch rode up to a cruel *alcalde* or major domo who really did oppress the helpless servitors and filled him full of lead. As a result, Sabida Quijano had plenty of friends along the river and also was able to anticipate the moves of peace officers seeking to run him down.

"Cullen Baker would make him an able lieutenant, only I can't see Baker playing second fiddle to anybody, that is if he really is alive," Slade remarked.

Captain Jim nodded. "Yes, Quijano has been raising plenty of hell," he observed. "He's got the men and if he manages to get enough guns to properly arm them he's liable to be in a position to stage raids like the one Cortinas made on Brownsville, when he took over the whole city and held it for forty-eight hours. Incidentally, we know Quijano got a shipment of rifle parts from Dallas recently, and that brings me back to Baker—he's alive, all right. Twice he's been reported by people who should know what they are talking about as being around the Big Hickory Bottoms, where Sam Bass and his bunch played hide-and-seek with peace officers for years. And the Bottoms aren't far from Dallas. I can't help but wonder if Baker is arranging arms shipments for Quijano and maybe convoying them to him."

"Could be," Slade conceded.

"Yep, could be," said Captain Jim. "Well, I've got a good man over there looking after things, Boyd Aitken."

"Aitken's a good man," Slade agreed.

"I received word from him that he believes he's got a line on the man who shipped that load to Quijano," Captain Jim added. "If he has, we should get some news from over there before long. I've nothing for you right now, Walt, I just thought you'd like to know about Baker."

"I'm glad you told me," Slade replied, adding grimly, "and if those reports are authentic, it puts Baker sort of in the category of unfinished business for me."

"Oh, well, maybe Aitken will finish it for you," said Captain Jim.

"I wouldn't be surprised," Slade agreed. "Boyd Aitken is a good ranger."

Walt Slade went back to his room and resumed what he had been working on when interrupted by the commander's summons. It consisted of some very intricate calculations contained in a textbook on higher mathematics.

Before joining the rangers, Slade had graduated from a famous college of engineering. His plan had been to take a postgraduate course to round out his technical education before going to work at his chosen profession. But his father had suffered business reversals, and successive droughts and blizzards had resulted in the loss of his cattle ranch. Soon afterward, the elder Slade died. All of which necessitated a revising of Walt Slade's plans. Captain Jim McNelty, with whom he had worked some during the summer vacations, suggested that Slade join the rangers while pursuing his studies in spare time. Slade did so. But ranger work had gotten a stronghold on him and he was loath to sever connections with the famous corps. He still planned to be an engineer and kept up his studies with that end in view. But he was young and there was plenty of time; he'd stick with the rangers for a while yet.

In the course of the years, Slade had built up a mixed reputation. To those who knew him as a ranger he was held in highest respect. The most fearless and ablest ranger of them all, was said of him. He had often worked under cover, sometimes without revealing his ranger connections. As a result, quite a few people, including some puzzled sheriffs, insisted that if El Halcon wasn't an owlhoot he missed being one by the skin of his teeth. Slade did nothing to discourage this erroneous viewpoint, having found it very useful at times in the course of his peace officer activities.

From time to time Slade would raise his eyes from his papers and think a bit on the unexpected "resurrection" of Cullen Baker. Slade was dubious about said resurrection. Notorious outlaws were always "coming to life." Plenty of folks insisted that Wyatt Earp never killed

Curly Bill Brocius at Iron Springs, that the Arizona out-law was seen in Mexico, years later, alive and well. The same could be said for John Wesley Hardin, Buckskin Frank Leslie, and others of similar ilk. Also, smaller fry had a habit of taking unto themselves the names of individuals outstanding in their dubious profession, especially if they happened to bear even a remote resemblance to the outlaw leader in question. Slade wouldn't be surprised if several Cullen Bakers showed up in various localities. No, he was not at all convinced that Cullen Baker had survived the wound he received on the bank of the Red River. Anyhow, if he was alive and was hanging around Dallas and the Big Hickory Bottoms country, there was an able man in the person of Boyd Aitken representing the rangers in that section, and Baker would very likely get his come-uppance. Slade went to bed with a peaceful mind.

But before dawn the telegraph wires would be clicking out a story of disaster and death.

Two

"HERE YOU ARE, boss, here you are! Sure cure for the mis'ry. Made by Mammy Jackson over in Big Hickory Bottoms. Mammy saw old Coffin-Head, the big rattle-snake, eat a yarb right after another snake bit him. She knew Coffin-Head was plumb full of mis'ry before he ate that yarb. But just as soon as he'd ate it he was peart as a sparrow on a limb. Mammy waited till Coffin-Head done crawl away, then she nosed around and found that yarb. She took it and ground it up and biled it down and put it in a bottle. This is one of the bottles, boss, and it's a sure cure for the mis'ry. Just four bits to make you feel fine and dandy."

The little Negro man's teeth flashed white in his black face as he waved the bottle ingratiatingly under the prospective customer's nose.

"Sure cure for the mis'ry!"

The man he accosted had "sailor" written all over him. He would have blended perfectly with the Corpus Cristi or Galveston waterfronts, but here in the heart of Dallas' "Deep Ellum" he was out of place as a seal in a prairie dog town.

Drowsing in the sunshine with its rows of drab "shot-gun" houses, yards bright with flowers, aged mammies rocking placidly on verandas, its peddlers, barbecue stands, places of amusement and crowds of busy, smiling black people, Deep Ellum was peaceful and serene. But when the lovely blue dusk stole over the prairie, the bon-fire stars of Texas blazed above and the answering lights brightened on Elm and Main Streets below, Deep Ellum had all the explosive potentialities of a cartload of nitroglycerin on a corduroy road.

The sailor fumbled a coin from his pocket, looking the little black man up and down speculatively. He was apparently satisfied with what he saw and arrived at a decision.

"Reckon I might as well have a bottle," he said. "I've been bothered with miseries of late."

The Negro man pocketed the half-dollar and handed over the bottle.

"This'll cure 'em, this'll cure 'em," he declared, grinning broader than ever.

The sailor stowed away the bottle. His eyes continued to speculate on the salesman. L

"By the way," he said, "you happen to know where I could locate a feller named Tol Grundy?"

Abruptly the grin vanished. The little Negro rolled his eyes till only the whites were visible.

"You-all mean that little old one-eyed white man who runs the shop over t'other side Good Street by the T & P Railroad yards?" he asked in a low mutter. "Boss, you stay away from that feller, he's a cunjer man if there ever was one. He'll put a spell on you, one that even Mammy Jackson can't take off."

"Reckon I'll risk it," replied the sailor. "Sounds like the feller I want to see, all right. Straight ahead, you say, and by the railroad yards?"

He nodded and walked on with his peculiar rolling gait. The Negro man removed his tattered hat and scratched his head. He shook the head dubiously, then abruptly he perked up.

"Here you are, gents, sure cure for the mis'ry."

But the three men to whom he proffered his wares brushed past without sparing him a glance. Their gaze was fixed on the sailor rolling along a few paces ahead.

Under the shadow of low-drawn, broad-brimmed hats

their faces were lean and bronzed. They wore "store clothes," but the black silk neckerchiefs looped about sinewy throats and the fancily stitched high-heel boots showing beneath their trousers bespoke the rangeland.

The keen-eyed little Negro noticed their intent regard of the sailor. For a moment he hesitated, staring after the retreating trio. Then, his curiosity aroused, he shuffled along in their wake.

Suddenly one of the following trio turned and glanced over his shoulder, the light from a shop window falling full on a scarred face. The little Negro's eyes widened.

"Lawdy! Lawdy!" he gulped in his throat. "It's *him!* Him or his ghost. Man, oh, man! Business is sure going to pick up!"

He hesitated, but curiosity drew him on.

The sailor walked slowly, past second-hand stores, pool halls and cafes. He glanced into windows where everything from threadbare cloth-of-gold evening gowns to folding bathtubs were displayed alongside "wish-ful-filments," love potions, magnetic lodestones for poker players and "van-van oil" to "shake the jinx." Pitchmen hawked their wares, street evangelists exhorted, often unnoticed by the swirling crowds. Beggars whined for alms.

The sailor moved on toward Good Street. On his left showed the winking lights of the railroad yards. A long freight train stood ready to pull out, its great locomotive hissing and panting like an angry monster aroused for action. He paused outside a dingy shop on the window of which was legended,

TOL GRUNDY—GENERAL MERCHANDISE

The sailor walked through the open door, peering around the dimly lit interior.

The three men who trailed him quickened their steps.

They, too, paused outside the door, fumbling with their black neckerchiefs.

Across the street, two men standing in the shadows tensed to hair-trigger alertness.

The sailor walked to the counter spanning the room, behind which stood a wizened man of uncertain age. He had one eye, bright as a snake's, a sharp nose and a long blue chin. His hair was grizzled and stood up like the bristles of a well-worn scrubbing brush.

"Reckon you're Tol Grundy," the sailor grunted interrogatively. "Must be, from the cut of your jib. Uh-huh, you must be Grundy."

"Well?" rumbled the man behind the counter in a voice deep and powerful and utterly at variance with his appearance.

"I'm from Sabida Quijano," said the sailor.

Grundy was taciturn.

"Got the stuff?"

"Uh-huh."

"Hand it over."

"I want a receipt first. You know Quijano."

"You'll get it."

The sailor fumbled a tightly wrapped package from his pocket, but he still held on to it. Grundy muttered something under his breath, reached beneath the counter and producd pen, ink and paper. He bent over the sheet. The sailor watched him, then glanced up at a slight sound behind him and stiffened as if struck by paralysis.

Grundy also glanced up and went rigid. Standing just inside the door were three masked men, eyes glinting in the shadow of low hatbrims. Each held a cocked gun.

The sailor swallowed, making a queer choking sound in his throat. Grundy stood motionless, his one eye glittering, his mouth a thin line above his blue chin.

The three gunmen glided forward.

"Turn around," one said harshly to the sailor. The seaman obeyed. The tall leader snatched the wrapped package from his hand and flipped it into his own pocket.

"Don't move," he warned. The three began backing toward the door. A voice rang out behind them.

"Elevate!"

The three whirled as a unit. Facing them were two men who also held drawn guns. There was an instant of crawling inaction. Then the room exploded to a roar of six-shooters. Red flashes gushed back and forth. Clouds of blue powder smoke swirled in the dim light. Tol Grundy went sideways from the counter and came up clutching a cocked sawed-off shotgun. A slug took it squarely on the stock and knocked it from his hands. Both barrels let go with a crashing roar. The double charge of buckshot smashed the window to splinters.

Outside, people scattered and fled with yells of terror. When two men, guns in hand, leaped over three sprawled bodies and into the street, not a man, woman or child was in sight.

The two men bounded across the street and headed for the railroad yards, where the long freight was rumbling slowly westward. Tol Grundy appeared in the doorway and fired six shots after them. Mumbling curses, he turned back to the store. Three dead and one desperately wounded man lay on the floor. The walls were pitted with bullet holes. The hanging lamp was swinging and guttering, held by one chain. Wind whistled through the gaping window.

Five minutes later the whole section swarmed with peace officers, searching, questioning. The sheriff of the county and a couple of deputies took over. They glanced at the two dead men lying just inside the door and swore bitterly.

"It's Marshal Skelton," said the sheriff. "Who's this feller beside him?"

One of the deputies turned the body over on its back. The dead man's coat fell open. Pinned to his shirt front was a silver star set on a silver circle, the badge of the Texas Rangers.

"What *did* bust loose here?" the sheriff demanded of nobody in particular. He glanced at the dead sailor, stepped across his sprawled body and knelt beside the wounded man, who was gasping and groaning as his life drained away through his shattered lungs.

"Who are you, feller, and what's this all about?" the sheriff demanded harshly. "Who was with you in this?"

"G-go to—" gurgled through the blood bubbling from the lips.

"*You're* going, and going fast," the sheriff replied. "Come clean before you cash in."

"I ain't talking!"

"Why not? You got nothing to lose."

"Agin my perfession. Go—to—to—"

The words ended in a gush of blood. The man's chest arched mightily as he fought for air. It sank in, and did not rise again. The sheriff got to his feet.

"Considerable of a man, anyhow," he growled with grudging admiration. He turned a bleak face to Tol Grundy, who was leaning against the counter nursing his bullet-gashed arm and looking rather sick.

"All right, Grundy," the sheriff said grimly. "I don't know what this is all about, but I do know that two law officers just died here in your store—a town marshal and a Texas Ranger. You got some explaining to do, Grundy."

The storekeeper replied instantly. "I ain't got nothing to worry about. I'll tell you all I know, which ain't much. This feller here—" he gestured to the dead sailor, "was bringing me a package. That dead hellion who just cashed in and two more came in with guns and grabbed the package. I tried to help down those three devils.

There's my shotgun over there by the wall, with the butt plate knocked off and a hole in the stock."

"What was in the package?'" demanded the sheriff.

"Opals, Mexican black opals," Grundy replied without hesitation. "About fifty thousand dollars worth."

"Who'd they come from?"

"From Sabida Quijano, the Mexican revolution jigger down in *mañana* land."

"Revolution jigger!" snorted the sheriff. "He's just an infernal Border bandit. Keep talking."

"Quijano sent me word a couple of weeks back that he was sending them by this feller, for me to buy or dispose of for him," Grundy added.

"Smuggled, eh?"

"Reckon so," Grundy agreed readily. "Can't see Quijano paying duty on anything. I don't know and I don't care. None of my business. Oh, I know it's against the law, but folks down along the Border don't get overly het up about it."

The sheriff was forced to admit this was true. He knew that many a prosperous and respected Border businessman got his start that way.

"Well, you kicked up one fine ruckus, for fair," he growled. "I'd ought to throw you in the calaboose for something, only I don't know just what. Did you get a look at those two sidewinders who got away?"

Grundy shook his head. "They had their hatbrims pulled down and handkerchiefs over their faces. I didn't see anything much but eyes and guns. They were both tall, but one was taller than the other one. Considerable over six foot, I'd say. They must have trailed the sailor up here from down around the Border or one of the Gulf ports, or had word sent them he was bringing the stuff. They couldn't have just guessed it. I've a notion they were cowhands, even though they were wearing store clothes, but I ain't sure."

"Did you see which way they went when they left here?" the sheriff asked.

"Uh-huh," Grundy answered. "They headed for the railroad yards."

The sheriff considered a moment, eyeing Grundy suspiciously, but apparently deciding that the storekeeper was telling the truth.

"Go out and get some of the boys and search the yards," he ordered one of his deputies, "Chances are you won't find anything, but we can't afford to miss any bets. There is going to be a mess over this, especially when Captain McNelty hears about it and learns one of his rangers got killed. Wonder how in blazes *they* knew what was up, or did he and Skelton just happen along?"

"They came in like they knew just what was going on," Grundy offered. "I've a notion maybe the rangers were keeping an eye on the sailor, too, or knew he was to show up here. Funny, though, that the rangers would mix up in it. Smuggling is usually looked after by the Federal men, and that's all they could have pinned on the sailor."

"Quijano has been causing plenty of trouble along the Border," the sheriff replied. "The rangers are keeping an eye on *him*, and fifty thousand *pesos* would buy a lot of guns and ammunition, and that's just what they don't want him to have. That's why I wish I could figure some way to lock you up, Grundy. By dealing with that riff-raff you're just plain helping him to kill folks down there."

Grundy shrugged his scrawny shoulders. "Well, you don't have to worry about me dealing with him any more," he said. "Tonight's cured me. I like to make money as well as anybody else, but not enough to look into gun barrels to get it."

The sheriff didn't look impressed. "Come on, Barnes,

and let's look those two bodies over," he said to the remaining deputy.

The pockets of the dead outlaw revealed nothing to which the sheriff attached any significance. The sailor's body appeared equally barren until the deputy drew from an inner pocket a flat bottle filled with some dark liquid. A plain white label was gummed to the glass and on it was a rude drawing of a rattlesnake posed to strike.

"Just some of Mammy Jackson's rattlesnake cure for the mis'ry," he grunted. "Nothing but sugar water, but the old folks believe in it. Might as well throw it away."

"No," the sheriff differed. "Hang on to it and everything else we took off these horned toads. We'll put it all together for McNelty to look over. Captain Jim is a mighty smart man and he's got smart men working with him who see things where ordinary folks don't. Can't tell. This bottle might mean something to them."

The sheriff was right.

Three

DEEP ELLUM is used to unusual appearing characters, but the man who sauntered along the narrow streets a few days later caused heads to turn.

More than six feet, he had shoulders and a chest to match his height. He wore the homely garb of the rangeland as Richard of the Lion Heart must have worn armor. Double cartridge belts encircled his lean waist and from the carefully worked and oiled cut-out holsters protruded the plain black butts of heavy guns.

The man's face was as arresting as his figure. His deeply bronzed, high-nosed countenance with its wide mouth and lean, powerful jaw was dominated by gay, reckless gray eyes that looked out upon the world and found it good.

Before he had been in the section ten minutes a whisper ran from cabin to cabin and shop to shop—

"That's Mistuh Walt Slade, the singingest man in Texas and the best shot! Uh-huh, that's The Hawk— El Halcon, the Mexicans call him."

"Outlaw feller, ain't he?"

"Dunno. Lots of folks say he is, but ain't nothing ever been proved on him. Ain't no lawman ever throwed *him* in the calaboose. Uh-huh, he's killed folks, but 'pears those folks always needed a killing powerful bad. He's a mighty nice feller—real buchrah—good to poor folks and always helping somebody that needs help. All the time showing up where there's trouble, and after he gets in a few licks, trouble just naturally grows wings and flies away. Uh-huh, he's a plumb nice feller, but man, oh man, don't get him het up! Better to give old Coffin-Head first holt and first bite!"

Walt Slade strolled along Deep Ellum's long and narrow streets, humming softly to himself in his musical voice, pausing to glance into shop windows, his flashing white smile answering the friendly nods in his direction from time to time. Finally he halted at a dingy little store that featured charms, voodoo signs and weird remedies for various ailments. The fat and cheerful proprietor greeted him smilingly as he entered.

"Something I can do for you?" he asked.

"Been having a mis'ry in my stomach of late," Slade told him gravely. "Reckon you got something that's good for it?"

"I got some powdered snake livers that's good for ordinary mis'ry," the proprietor returned. "But, if you got a plumb bad mis'ry, what you need is a bottle of Mammy Jackson's mis'ry cure. That's a plumb sure cure."

"That's fine," Slade replied. "I've heard of that. I'll take a bottle."

The shopkeeper shook his head. "Boss, I ain't got none of that cure," he admitted. "Mammy Jackson don't let nobody but Little Mose Wagner sell that cure for her. Mose is a cunjer-marked man and can't put no spell on that cure."

"Where can I find Little Mose?" Slade asked.

"You go right down Ellum Street and you'll find Little Mose. He'll be selling cures down around the corner of Good Street about this time in the evening."

Slade thanked the proprietor, bought a cunjer charm and departed. As he walked along Elm Street he drew from his pocket a flat bottle with a rude drawing of a rattlesnake on the plain white label. It was the bottle of mis'ry cure Sheriff Pres Dawes had taken from the sailor killed in Tol Grundy's store. Slade had congratulated the sheriff on saving it.

"It might provide the very lead we need," he said. "The sailor must have bought it from somebody the night he was killed, and he didn't buy it to cure a mis'ry. He bought it for an excuse to ask some questions of somebody. I want to try and find the man who sold it to him."

As Slade neared Good Street, he heard Little Mose Wagner's chant.

"Sure cure for the mis'ry, folks! Just four bits a bottle."

Slade paused beside the little Negro, smiling down at him from his great height. He gravely accepted a bottle, handed Little Mose a silver dollar and declined change. Little Mose grinned delightedly, his eyes widening in recognition. Slade continued to smile down at him.

"By the way, Mose," he said, "two or three nights back did you happen to sell a bottle of misery cure to a sailor-looking fellow?"

The grin left Little Mose's face and Little Mose got ready to "know nothin'."

But something in the steady gaze of the long gray eyes, and perhaps the things he had heard whispered about this tall man with the bronzed face, changed his mind for him.

"Yes, sir, I reckon I did," he admitted in low tones.

"A fellow who went and got himself killed in Tol Grundy's store right after you sold him the misery cure?"

"Boss, I dunno," Little Mose said. "I didn't see that sailor feller after he got himself killed. I don't look at no dead folks if I can help it. Maybe it was the same feller, but the mis'ry cure didn't have anything to do with it, boss. I told that sailor feller that Tol Grundy was a cunjer man and he'd best stay away from him, but he wouldn't listen. He went right into that man's store."

Slade nodded. Little Mose had evidently kept an eye on the sailor as he made his way to Grundy's store.

"Happen to see two or three men going in with him?" he asked casually.

Little Mose shook his head vigorously. "He went in by himself," he declared. He hesitated, his forehead wrinkling. Slade waited patiently.

"Uh-huh, he went in by himself," Little Mose repeated, "but three fellers who were taggin' along after him went in, too, right after he did. And then two more fellers who were standing in the dark across the street, they went in, too. Mighty fast. And then the big bobberty busted loose."

Slade nodded, and asked the question the answer to which he was most desirous of getting.

"The three fellows who were tagging after the sailor, did you get a look at them?"

Again Little Mose hesitated, drew a deep breath, eyed Slade a moment, and took the plunge.

"Uh-huh, I got a look at them, but I didn't look overly close. They were all three tall fellers, but one was a sight taller than the other two. He wasn't as tall as you, boss, but he was plenty high off the ground. He had a cuttin' mark on his face, on the right side. Bad looking cuttin' mark, from his eye across toward his ear."

Slade nodded again and considered a moment.

"Mose," he said suddenly, "do you happen to remember what was going on in the railroad yards about the time of the big bobberty?"

"What you mean going on, boss?"

Slade explained, "Was there a freight train pulling out or about ready to pull out at the time?"

"Yes, sir, there was," Mose replied. "The westbound

highball was pulling out right then. I know it was the highball by the way Mistuh Brewster, the engineer, blowed the whistle. He lives right over on Swiss Avenue and when he pulls out on his run he whistles his wife a funny little tootle-toot-toot. I know Mistuh Brewster and I always pay mind to that whistle-bye-bye of his. Yes, sir, it was the highball pulling out right then, just starting to move slow, hadn't got the main-lead switch light when the shooting started."

"Would have taken him several minutes to begin getting up speed?" Slade asked.

"Uh-huh," nodded Mose. "He'd got the white light onto the lead, but he wouldn't get the main light till his caboose cleared onto the lead. Don't make no speed till he gets that white light on the main line."

Slade slipped another dollar into Little Mose's palm.

"Any notion where I could find that engineer?" he asked.

"Well, sir," said Little Mose, pocketing the dollar, "I'd say you could find him at home right about now. This is his day in town. He don't pull out again till tomorrow night. Like for me to take you over to his place?"

"That would be fine."

"Then come along, boss," said Little Mose, picking up his bag of bottles. "We'll get there in a jiffy."

A pretty young woman opened the door when Slade knocked at the trim little cottage where the engineer lived.

"Why, hello, Mose," she greeted the cure peddler. She cast an inquiring glance at Slade.

"Miss Rose, this gentleman would like to speak to Mistuh John about something," Mose explained.

"Come right in, sir," Mrs. Brewster invited. "My husband will be glad to see you. Come in, Mose."

"No, ma'am," Mose declined. "I gotta get back to my business." He replaced his tattered hat and ambled off.

John Brewster proved to be a pleasant-faced man of middle age. He greeted Slade cordially and offered him a chair.

"Sorry to disturb you, sir," Slade said, "but I'd like to ask you a question. Last Wednesday night, on your run west out of Dallas, did anything out of the ordinary happen?"

"Why, yes," the engineer replied. "How'd you guess it? Just outside the city limits, about where the Brazos Trail crosses the right-of-way, some hobo, wanting to get off, I reckon, turned an air-hose angle cock and came close to wrecking us. Would have, I guess, if we'd been going a little faster. As it was, it's a wonder we didn't pull a couple of drawbars. It took the brakeman twenty minutes to find that closed cock and open it so we could get going. It sure slammed the brakes on when that fool closed the valve. Stuck 'em all along the train. They had to bleed the air on nearly every car to get the brakes released."

"You didn't see who did it?"

The engineer shook his head. "No, it was dark," he explained. "Things like that happen every now and then, though seldom does a 'bo slam the valve shut that way. You a railroad detective?"

"No," Slade smiled as he stood up, "but I'm sort of interested in what happened. Much obliged, sir, you did me a good turn."

He said goodbye to the engineer and his wife and headed back into Deep Ellum.

What he had learned substantiated the conclusion he had already arrived at. The two killers had caught the fast freight out of town, getting off where the railroad crossed the Brazos Trail. Doubtless they had horses waiting for them nearby. Slade was convinced that it was the same two men who stopped the train. No bumper-riding hobo would have slammed the air-hose valve shut like that. He would have closed it slowly so as to apply the brakes gradually. Then when he'd slowed the train down sufficiently to make it safe for him to unload, he'd have opened the cock again. A real hobo would have had no desire to attract attention to himself by stopping the fast freight and possibly de-railing it. It was really a wonder the two bandits didn't wreck the train and kill themselves. But fifty thousand dollars' worth of opals!

Slade wondered if there was more to the business than showed on the surface. The storekeeper, Tol Grundy, had freely admitted that they came from Sabida Quijano. Just why was Quijano sending them all the way to Dallas, way up in the northeastern section of the state, to be disposed of, Slade wondered, and just what sort of a link was there between the Mexican bandit and the Dallas storekeeper? And where did the men who robbed and killed the sailor fit into the picture? And who *were* those men, or one of them?

Slade turned into a dark and narrow side street he and Mose had traversed on their way to the engineer's house. On either side were silent, unlighted buildings and shacks. The openings between the buildings were like black cave mouths. The street lighting was inadequate and he picked his way carefully over the rough and broken pavement.

Suddenly a frantic yell shattered the silence.

"Look out, boss! Look out!" Slade recognized the voice of Little Mose Wagner. Instantly he hurled himself down.

From a black and narrow opening between two buildings gushed a streak of reddish fire. The twin roars of a shotgun split the air.

Prone on the ground, Slade snapped both guns from their sheaths and sent trace bullets toward the opening. He heard the bullets thud against the wall, heard a clang as of smitten metal, the clatter of something falling and a yelp of pain. He fired twice more at the sound, scrambled to his feet and leaped forward, a cocked gun in each hand. He reached the opening and fired again into the darkness. He thought he heard a patter of running feet. He peered into the opening. A faint glow from the skyline beyond filtered the shadows but he could see nothing. He tried to enter the crack but found it would not accommodate his breadth of shoulders. It must have been a mighty scrawny individual who holed up in the narrow opening. His foot struck against something that clattered on the cobbles. He stooped and picked up the object. It was a double-barreled sawed-off shotgun.

From nearby sounded Mose Wagner's anxious voice. "You all right, boss?"

"Yes, thanks to you, Mose," Slade replied. "Where are you?"

"Here I am," replied the little Negro from another narrow opening. "Come on, boss, come on; there'll be lawmen around here in a jiffy. Come on, follow me."

Trailing Little Mose, Slade found himself in the alley back of the street. In the distance sounded cries drawing nearer.

"I knew all that shooting would bring folks," babbled Little Mose.

They reached another alley narrower and darker than the first. Down this Little Mose pattered, Slade crowding close behind him. Mose paused a few minutes later, there was the rattle of a key in a lock, a door creaked open.

"Inside," he whispered. As soon as Slade was through the door, he closed and locked it.

"Stand still till I get the lamp lighted," he warned.

A light flared up, revealing a spotlessly clean room fitted up with a stove, two bunks built against the walls, a table and a couple of chairs.

"Now we're all set," chuckled Mose. "Just a minute and I'll get the coffee pot goin'. And there's a pot of greens and chitlin's ready to heat up, and corn pone in the oven. Grab a chair and take a load off your feet."

Slade sat down and glanced around the room with interest. His eyes fixed on a big high-pommeled saddle hanging on a peg. Little Mose noticed his gaze and chuckled.

"Yep, I used to be a cowhand," he said. "Used to ride for the Forked S up north of here. Lots of Negro cowboys in that section. I still keep me a horse in Pork-chest Brady's stable down the lane a piece. I like to ride but I got sort of stove up in a stampede and ain't much good for range work any more. That's how come I'm here in town selling mis'ry cure. I work over in the cotton gin, too, when they're busy. I make out."

Slade nodded, his gray eyes smiling. "How come you to spot that drygulcher?" he asked.

"Boss," Mose replied, "when I left Mistuh Brewster's house after you went in with Miss Rose, I saw that feller standing across the street watching the house. He was wearing a big long coat wrapped around him and had his hat pulled down. He had something under the coat. Reckon it was that shotgun you picked up. I figured that feller wasn't up to no good, so I moseyed down the street a little ways and holed up. I saw you come out of the house and that feller he snuck along behind you, quite a ways back. When you turned into Boone Street where it was good and dark, that feller he slid in between two buildings. I knew he was headed for the alley, so I snuck in behind him. He went up that alley mighty fast to get ahead of you, and crawled in between those two warehouses. So I scooted for the street to get ahead of you, but I fell over a crate in that crack and came mighty nigh to being too late. When I saw you just passing, I yelped."

Slade reached out his slender bronzed hand and he and

Little Mose shook. Then while Mose got busy with the coffee and the greens, Slade examined the shotgun. It was a good make of sporting gun, the barrels cut off short with a hacksaw. A wicked weapon and lethal.

He told Mose, "My slug hit right on the lock and knocked one hammer off. Hope it took a section of his hand off, but he didn't yelp like he was hurt much."

" 'Pears somebody hereabouts don't like you overly well," Little Mose commented.

Slade gazed at the shotgun stock, his black brows drawing together until the concentration furrow was deep between them.

"Mose," he asked suddenly, "do you notice anything funny looking about this scattergun?"

Little Mose took the weapon. "Stock's brand new," he remarked. "Rest of the gun ain't, but the stock is."

"So I figure," Slade said. "Somehow I've got a notion this isn't the first time this thing has stopped lead. Have a feeling that jigger used it before. Killer gun, all right."

"Cunjer-man gun!" grunted Little Mose as he spread the table with a snowy cloth. By the time he had placed knives, forks, and spoons with great nicety, the greens and chitlin's were ready, the coffee bubbling. Both drew up chairs and a period of busy silence followed.

Slade drained a final cup of coffee, fished out the makin's and rolled cigarettes for himself and his companion.

"Mose," he said, "have you any notion where those two men you saw the other night hole up, the ones who went into Tol Grundy's store?"

Little Mose rolled his eyes. "I reckon," he replied slowly, "that they're mighty apt to hole up over in Big Hickory Bottoms."

Slade regarded Mose a moment.

"What makes you think so?" he asked.

Mose hesitated before replying. "I got reasons," he said at length. He took another swallow of coffee. Then his brown eyes met Slade's gaze steadily.

"Boss," he said, "do you figure to go after those two fellers?"

"Yes."

Mose wrinkled his forehead again. He said, "You'd best leave those fellers alone. They're powerful bad."

Slade remained silent.

"Boss, that tall feller with the scar alongside his eye is the ghost man, Cullen Baker!"

Four

WALT SLADE STARED at the little Negro.

"Boss, I know what you're thinking!" Little Mose exclaimed. "You're thinking what a lot of folks thought, that a ranger feller killed Cullen Baker up by the Red River. Ranger feller shot him, all right, but he didn't kill him. Old Cullen fell in the river, or maybe he jumped in. He's a powerful swimmer, ain't no better. He swum under water and drifted with the current. Had a hole spang through him, but maybe the cold water stopped the bleeding."

Slade could understand that. Doubtless the icy waters of the storm-swollen Red had a certain astringent effect, and men can be shot through and survive providing no vital organ is pierced and no large vein or artery severed.

"You don't think the ranger killed Cullen Baker, then?" he asked.

"No, sir, he didn't," Little Mose declared. "Leastwise old Cullen is still walking around, and that wasn't the first time Cullen Baker swam away from a killing. Happened once before when his brother-in-law, the feller he tried to hang, gunned him over by the Black Water in Big Hickory Bottoms. That's how Cullen got that scar alongside his eyes. He jumped into the Black Water that time. Everybody was sure he was done for—hadn't anybody ever swum the Black Water. It's full of trailing vines and roots that catches a man and holds him tight till he drowns. But Cullen Baker swam it. He was mighty bad hurt but he got to Mammy Jackson's cabin and made her patch him up and feed him. Reckon he'd have killed

35

her if she'd been anybody else but Mammy Jackson.
Mammy don't kill easy. 'Sides, everybody knows that
anybody who killed Mammy Jackson would tromp the
world like a lonesome wind and never, never find rest."

Mose paused, glanced around the cabin, his eyes rolling. His voice dropped to a whisper.

"Yes, Mammy Jackson cured him that time," he
added. "She saved his life. But there's folks that say she
took his soul for pay. They say old Cullen ain't got no
soul no more, and that's why nobody can kill him."

Slade gazed curiously at Little Mose. He was convinced that Mose Wagner was a brave man, but now his
hands were trembling, his black face beaded with sweat.
Not that there was anything unusual about it. Hardy
men who fear no mortal foe will sometimes shake with
terror at the shadows of their own minds.

"And after Cullen Baker got out of the Red River and
his wound healed up, where did he go?" Slade asked.

"Went down into Mexico," Mose replied.

"Sure about that?"

"Yes, boss, I'm sure. Bully Evans saw him down there
and Bully knew Cullen well as I do. That's why Bully
left Mexico and come back up here. He had a good job
in Mexico, but he didn't 'low to stick around close to
Cullen Baker. He knew that Cullen Baker don't like us
folks."

Slade nodded. He knew that Cullen Baker, before he
really turned outlaw, had been jailed during one of his
drinking sprees. The guard at the jail was a Negro. After
Baker was released he returned and killed the Negro
guard and became an outlaw.

One of Baker's most audacious and cruel exploits occurred when he, posing as another man, organized a
posse of Negroes to hunt Baker, their hated enemy. He
drilled the Negroes with dummy guns and finally led
sixteen of them to meet a squad of his own outlaws. He

brought the two squads together, for the purpose of further drilling them, he explained. He commanded, "Load! Aim! Fire!" His outlaws' guns were not dummies and the helpless and unsuspecting Negroes were shot down to a man.

"And you're sure, Mose, that the man you saw the other night was Cullen Baker? Perhaps you thought it was Baker because of the scar you mentioned, which could have been just one similar to the scar Baker wears."

Little Mose shook his head. "Nope, I wasn't making any mistake," he replied. "I wasn't paying any attention to the scar, I just mentioned it when I was telling you what the feller looked like. I've known Cullen Baker for ten years, maybe more. Knew him before he got to be a real owlhoot. He was always a ruckus-raising man who didn't like nobody. Old Cullen always was a hater, I reckon. Notion he don't even like himself. Yes, it was Cullen Baker, all right, nobody else."

For some minutes Slade sat smoking. There appeared to be little doubt that Cullen Baker was alive. The worst outlaw Texas had ever known. A man utterly ruthless, audaciously courageous, without mercy. And a man with a quick mind, a cold, clear-thinking brain that sized up a situation with hair-trigger alertness and almost invariably did the right thing. Witness, his exploit on the Red River. Slade's last glimpse of the outlaw had been a hand raised above the water in what was apparently the hopeless gesture of a drowning man. Which of course was the impression Baker wanted to give. And a moment later he had evidently been swimming under the surface with the current to help him quickly vanish in the deepening gloom of evening.

What gave Slade most cause for concern was the apparent tie-up between Baker and the Mexican Border bandit, Sabida Quijano. Slade knew that Quijano was a man whose only desire was to live high on the proceeds of his depredations. Quijano would make a rich haul in cattle or stolen gold or from smuggled goods, and he and his followers would proceed to immediately dissipate the loot in riotous living, and when it was gone set out on another marauding expedition with the sole aim of replenishing their coffers. And Quijano operated mostly in Mexico making only occasional raids north of the Border. He had so far been looked upon by the rangers and other Texas peace officers as more of a nuisance than anything else.

But Quijano had a numerous following, and around the hard core of his daring, straight shooting and well-equipped outlaws a large and really dangerous force could be quickly assembled, providing the necessary arms were forthcoming.

Not that Slade feared that Quijano would exert himself to make any such attempt. Left alone, he would be content to play the role of a self-centered Robin Hood and continue to raise minor turmoil along the Rio Grande until he was finally eliminated.

But Cullen Baker might easily be a horse of a very different hue. Judging from his past history, Baker did have certain ambitions, ambitions motivated by vengeance. Slade believed nothing would please Baker better than to start a roaring conflagration along the Border that would give him opportunity to glut his vengeance to the full.

So what if Baker was plotting to depose Quijano and take over the leadership of the band in his stead? Baker would never be satisfied to play the role of a petty frontier outlaw if he could vision wider fields. And conditions south of the Rio Grande were admirably suited to just such an endeavor. The country was seething with unrest, especially in the great northern provinces of Sonora and Chihuahua. The old dictator who had for so long ruled Mexico with an iron hand was losing his grip, his throne was becoming shaky. In fact, Slade believed that a daring and able leader, such as Cullen Baker undoubtedly was, could set up an independent government in the north without great difficulty. And the thought of such a man as Cullen Baker, ruler of the vast stretch of country along the Rio Grande, gave Slade a cold feeling inside. ⌊

Tol Grundy, the Dallas storekeeper, was mixed up in the deal somehow. Just how, Slade wasn't sure. Grundy was acting, in a way, as a fence for Quijano, a receiver and disposer of unlawfully acquired property. But not in the real technical sense of the word. There was little doubt in Slade's mind that the opals had been smuggled into the country. And in any event, Grundy was in the clear. He had a perfect right to buy jewels from Quijano or anybody else and dispose of them at a profit. And he couldn't very well be required to investigate each purchase he might make and learn just where it came from or under what conditions. He had frankly admitted to the sheriff of Dallas county that it was quite likely that the opals were smuggled, but that was none of his business. No, there was nothing on Grundy that could be made to stand up in court. ⌊

The important question was just what was back of Cullen Baker's seizure of the jewels. Was there a doublecross somewhere? Was Baker working the double-cross on Quijano? Slade was inclined to doubt it. The value of the opals, while large, was hardly sufficient to cause Baker to abandon what was very likely a contact and an alliance potentially worth much more to him than the money the opals represented.

And what appeared to be but a routine chore of running down and eliminating another owlhoot pest abruptly loomed as something of possible international importance. And if Little Mose was right in his insistence that Baker hung out somewhere in the Big Hickory Bottoms, the task was not going to be easy.

But Cullen Baker had killed a Texas Ranger. To which Captain McNelty gave first thought when he dispatched his ace-man to avenge the murder of Ranger Boyd Aitken. Slade experienced a feeling of acute pain as he thought of the bluff, kindly and generous Aitken, a man of high courage and high principles and extremely likeable.

Little Mose Wagner's gaze was fixed on the bleak face of El Halcon, for at the moment Walt Slade did strangely resemble the fierce mountain hawk that was utterly fearless and powerful enough to give battle to an eagle, and perfectly willing to do just that. Slade's normally sunny eyes were now devoid of laughter and coldly gray.

"Boss," Little Mose quavered, "are you really going into the swamps after Cullen Baker?"

Slade nodded. Little Mose gulped in his throat.

"Now we both done for! Those swamps are full of devils, boss, and once they get hold of us they won't never let go!"

"What do you mean 'us'?" Slade asked.

" 'Cause I've got to go along if you're going," groaned Little Mose. "You'd get plumb lost before you'd gone a mile. No man who don't know the swamps and the Bottoms can find his way around in there. Me, I was born and brought up in the Bottoms and I know 'em, so I got to go along to show you the way."

Walt Slade chuckled, his eyes filled with admiration for the little man who, admitting his own terrible fears, was nevertheless grimly determined to do what he thought the right thing. Here, Slade knew, was genuine courage. He reached over and patted Little Mose's scrawny shoulder.

"It appears that when the Good Lord goes in for the

making of a *real* man, He doesn't pay much mind to what color He paints him," he smiled.

"Maybe not," sighed Little Mose, "but just the same, I'm scared!"

His eyes roamed around the cabin and centered on a guitar hanging on the wall.

"Boss," he said, "I heard tell you're a powerful singin' man. I got a notion that if you'd just sing me a song or two I'd feel a heap better."

Slade took the guitar, tuned it to his liking and ran his fingers over the strings with crisp power. Then he threw back his black head and his voice pealed forth in a song he had heard the Negroes sing in the cotton fields and on the levees, a song of weird, haunting beauty.

> Where the white magnolias blossom,
> And the waxen ghost flowers grow
> And the bayou waters ripple
> And the sighin' breezes blow,
> There I'm goin', for I'm lonesome,
> And I'm weary, trompin' home,
> For I drank the bayou water
> And no matter where I roam,
> Still I hear the swamplands callin',
> And I hear the swamp birds cry,
> With their voices everlastin',
> Like the stars up in the sky.
> Yes, I drank the bayou water
> And I never can be free
> From those swampland voices callin'
> In the night time, callin' me!

Little Mose sat entranced. And when the music ended in a crash of chords, he squared his shoulders and lifted his head.

"Boss," he said, "when you sing like that, I get chills

and fever all up and down my backbone, but I ain't scared no more. I ain't scared to go anywhere with a man who can sing that way.

"And now," he added, "you'd better stay right here tonight. Comfortable bed over there, and we got baked spareribs and hot biscuits for breakfast. We'll start out for Big Hickory early. Take us all day to get there."

"I think you've got the right notion, Mose," Slade conceded, "and I could stand a little shut-eye right now."

Dawn found both astir. After breakfast they set out. Wagner's mount proved to be a rangy bay that heightened Slade's respect for Little Mose's judgment of horse flesh. And when Wagner's eyes fell on Shadow, he shook his head in admiration.

"The sort of a horse a feller dreams about but don't never expect to see," he declared.

"Yes, old Shadow is quite a horse," Slade agreed.

The sun was low in the western sky when they at last sighted from the crest of a rise, the vast and desolate region of the swampland bottoms.

As far as the eye could reach were wide stretches of lonely, death-breeding swamp relieved by ponds of black and peaty water that, mirror-like, flashed up red rays from the setting sun. The dying light of evening played on the surface of reed-fringed lagoons as a faint breeze stirred the shadows. The heavens above were filled with wild fowl streaming with flashes of flying gold and the lurid stain of blood.

Farther on were patches of forest, the lofty trees covered for the most part with a dense growth of a species of ochella moss.

There was something singularly impressive about those great trees festooned from top to bottom with trailing wreaths of the sad-hued moss swaying gently in the wind. Slade shook his head as he gazed on the forbidding terrain, the foliage dense, the vines hanging in tangled masses.

Four or five Chickahominy swamps boiled down into one! Very likely it wouldn't get real daylight in there till noon. And Cullen Baker knew every foot of the section. With the Bottoms to hide in, and the prairies to the east and west to run in, when running was in order, it was a perfect hole-up for outlaws. Slade knew that Sam Bass and his train robbers played hide-and-seek with rangers, sheriffs and railroad detectives in this section for months, and weren't caught. He realized that if it wasn't for Little Mose to guide him and show him the trails he would stand scant chance of coming up with the outlaw. As it was, he had his work cut out for him.

Little Mose was speaking:

"Here is the Dark Empire of the haunts, Mistuh Slade. Here's where the Comanches used to burn folks at the stake while their cat-people run through the woods and mewed beneath the moon. Here's where the hobgoblins hang out and the voodoo folks come to work their spells. Reckon we ain't never going to get out of here, suh. Don't you let none of those branches or vines touch you when we get into the woods. They'll put a spell on you for certain, and you'll shrivel up or maybe turn black as I am."

"But you used to live in the Bottoms," Slade pointed out.

"Uh-huh, but that was when I was too young to have enough sense to be proper scared of haunts and cunjer folks," Little Mose replied gloomily. "Come on, boss, it'll be dark now before we get to Mammy Jackson's cabin over by the Black Water. Lawdy! Lawdy!"

They moved down the slope and entered the swampland, where the reeds were so tall they reached above their heads, mounted though they were. As the rising mists and the deepening shadows swallowed them, a watching horseman concealed in a thicket atop a distant rise pulled out and rode slowly toward the swamp.

Five

ALONG A BARELY PERCEPTIBLE winding track Little Mose
led the way. On either side was treacherous, quaking
soil. Quicksand. They passed deep and sullen pools, the
surfaces swirled and eddied by the passage of snakes and
other reptiles. Wading birds whirred up with strident
cries and a thunder of beating wings as they approached.
The wind stirred an eerie music through the reeds.

"There's a mean looking fellow over there," Slade
suddenly remarked, gesturing toward a big snake that
lay on a nearby log, glittering. "Swamp moccasin."

"That's what you think!" cried Little Mose. "That
ain't no swamp moccasin. That's one of Mammy
Jackson's spirits she puts out here to let her know who's
coming. Don't look him in the eye, boss. I know him
well, and so do lots of other folks. And don't you go
shooting at him, either. He'll turn the bullet spang back
at you."

Slade winked at the unimpressed snake.

They rode slowly, Little Mose peering ahead from
side to side. To Slade it seemed there was little to choose
from between the faint track and the paralleling soil, but
Little Mose cautioned him not to stray to either side.

"That mud ain't got no bottom," he declared. "And
what it takes hold of it don't let go. Follow close behind
me, boss."

However, it was the keen eyes of Slade that noted
what Little Mose did not.

"Horses have passed this way not long ago," he remarked, "quite a few of them. Also pack mules bearing
pack saddles well loaded with something."

"How do you know?" Little Mose asked wonderingly.

"Plenty of signs," Slade replied. "See that dangling twig over there? The break is not more than a couple of days old, I'd say. And ahead of it you'll see a palmetto frond pretty well stripped of leaves, with break marks where the stems were torn loose. And look close at that bare spot and you'll see the print of a horse's iron with the edges still clean-cut, not sloughed off as they would be if the mark was old. Right beside it is a narrower track that could only have been made by a mule shoe. The pack saddles—aparejos—bulge out from the mule's sides when they're loaded and brush against the twigs and fronds, breaking them and stripping them of leaves. Yes, quite a few loads of something have gone this way during the past few days."

Little Mose hauled off his hat and scratched his head, as does one who witnesses something beyond his understanding.

"When you point 'em out I can see those things," he said, "but I sure wouldn't never have noticed them by myself."

The sun vanished, the shadows deepened. Soon it was black and Mose called a halt. "Moon'll be up in a little bit," he said. "We'd best wait."

The swampland had been deathly silent when they entered it, the stillness broken only by the flight of startled birds, but with the closing down of night it was different. Bullfrogs boomed. Night-flying fowls uttered weird cries. There were mysterious sucking noises, caused, Slade imagined, by sinking areas of swamp and the bursting bubbles of foul, uprushing gases.

As the darkness deepened, strange lights played over the surface of the bog. Slade recognized them for will-o'-the-wisps or fen fire, but Mose had another explanation.

"Them's spirits of the dead," he whispered. "Spirits of bad folks that never, never find rest."

As Slade watched the marsh-born balls of fire roll this way and that, vapor-tossed and ever restless, he was almost inclined to agree, or at least to sympathize, with Little Mose. There was something uncannily life-like in their unceasing movement.

Suddenly the air was rent by a chorus of plaintive and heart-rending cries—human cries they seemed, the piercing wail of children in distress. As if all the babies since the world began were crying together. The very tree leaves seemed to shiver under the impact of that shivery symphony of hopeless distress.

The eerie whimpering ceased as suddenly as it began. Then there was a heavy splash in the water nearby and the cries started again with redoubled intensity. Little Mose moaned and shivered.

"Just alligators," Slade said. "Heave a rock in there and they'll bellow like a steer hung on a barbed-wire fence."

The east began to brighten, overhead the glowing stars paled. A line of silver fire appeared on the horizon and the full moon rose, casting a ghostly light over the desolate marshland.

"Let's get going, boss," said Little Mose. "Another mile and we'll be out of this mud and on good ground under the trees. The woods over there run clean to the prairie on the north."

They moved on, picking their way with care. The horses didn't like it and snorted and shivered.

"They can smell the haunts," declared Mose.

Slade, however, took the more practical view that the animals were uneasy because they sensed the deadly danger of the quicksand-like mud on either side of the narrow track. He himself experienced a feeling of relief when after another half hour had passed they were in the deeper gloom beneath the trees and the irons rang on solid and hard soil. Mose quickened his mount's pace.

"Nothing to be scared of now but haunts and swamp devils," he said. "All good going from here to Mammy Jackson's cabin. We'll be there in a jiffy."

They had covered two miles over firm ground when the trees thinned and a little clearing appeared. Bathed in the moonlight, stood a small, tightly built cabin.

"That's Mammy's shack," said Little Mose.

They dismounted in front of the cabin. Mose advanced and knocked timidly.

"Come in," said a deep musical voice inside the cabin. "Come in, Mose, and bring the white gentleman with you."

"Now how'd she know that, with the door tight shut?" whispered Little Mose. He hesitantly pushed open the door and they entered the cabin which was lighted by a bracket lamp.

Mammy Jackson sat on the far side of the room in front of a brightly burning fire, her back to the door. On the hearth sat a great black cat. Above the fireplace was a tame owl on a perch, regarding them with yellow and dubious eyes. Over the fire hung a big iron pot that gave off a rich and savory smell.

Mammy Jackson turned around. Her hair was snow-white, her face a myriad of wrinkles, but her black eyes were wonderfully bright and youthful and very wise.

"Pull up a chair, white gentleman, pull up a chair, Mose," she said. "Coffee's heating and there's a kettle of stew on the fire. We'll let it bubble a bit longer and then we'll eat."

Slade and Mose sat down, the latter glancing apprehensively at the owl and the cat.

"Mammy, this gentleman is looking for Cullen Baker."

Mammy Jackson did not appear surprised. "Reckon he'll find him, sooner or later," she said composedly. "Well, it's about time Cullen Baker was getting his come-uppance. There ain't no good in him, never was and never will be. Just a born trouble-maker is Cullen Baker."

Slade smiled down at the little old woman whom he instantly liked.

"Any notion where I can find him, Mammy?" he asked.

Mammy Jackson looked meditative. "Up to the north in the woods alongside the Black Water, there's an old cabin, or was one, once," she replied. "Cullen Baker used to hang out there when he was living in the Bottoms. He might be there now, if he hasn't ambled off someplace else. Anyhow, he passed this way with five other fellows a few days back, heading north, or so I was told."

"I told you that snake was a spirit, boss," Little Mose murmured under his breath.

Mammy Jackson smiled slightly but apparently took no heed of the remark.

"You know the trail up to that old cabin, Mose," she said. "It ain't much of a trail, even less than it used to be, but I reckon you can follow it. If you can't, I reckon Mistuh Slade can show you how."

"Now how'd she know *that!*" cried Little Mose. "I never said no names!"

Mammy Jackson laughed out loud, her laugh as musical as her voice.

"Mose," she said, "if you ever expect to get to be as old as I am, you'd better learn to listen close when folks talk about other folks and describe them and name their names."

Mose couldn't see anything humorous about the matter.

"Be ready to eat in a minute now," said Mammy. "I'll set the table."

She rose to her feet and began moving about the room. In the distance, an owl hooted with an unnatural screaming sort of note.

Mammy Jackson paused in her activities and her bright old eyes were fixed on the owl over the fireplace.

Suddenly the owl rose on his perch, mantling himself with his wings. At the same time the cat stood up and gazed fixedly at the door.

"Somebody's coming up the trail," said Mammy Jackson. "A long ways off, but he's coming."

"Ain't nobody got no business coming up that trail this time of night," muttered Mose.

Slade rose from his chair. "A back door to this cabin, Mammy?" he asked.

"Right through the room there. You can't miss it," replied Mammy Jackson.

Mose also stood up, but Slade halted him with a gesture. "You stay put," he ordered. "We can't afford any noise."

Slade glided into the dark back room.

He found the door without difficulty and slipped through it. He stole noiselessly around the cabin and darted across the moonlit clearing and into the shadow where he could command the trail. His ears caught the sound of slowly beating hoofs steadily drawing nearer. He waited.

The sound of pacing hoofs loudened. Another moment and a shadow loomed in an opening between the trees. It resolved into a mounted man, a rather small man wrapped in a long cloak. Slade's voice rang out.

"That'll be far enough, fellow. Elevate!"

The response was an instant and unexpected blaze of gunfire. Slade ducked, weaved and jerked his own guns as the approaching horse wheeled and went streaking back into the shadows. Slade's guns were out but there was nothing to shoot at. He paused to listen and when his ears stopped ringing he heard hoofbeats pounding into the distance.

The cabin door banged open. Little Mose came running, gun in hand.

"Hold it!" Slade told him.

"Did you get him, boss?" Little Mose panted to a halt and glared around.

"I fumbled that one, Mose. He must have had a gun in his hand. Before I could pull trigger he was gone into the dark. He sure hightailed, though."

Slade shook his head. He glided into the opening between the trees and searched the narrow trail carefully for more than a hundred yards, and found nothing. Disgusted, he returned to the clearing.

"Outsmarted, all right," he told Mose.

"Old Cullen Baker is sure smart and bad," said Mose.

"It wasn't Cullen Baker," Slade replied. "He was a small man wrapped in a big cloak."

"The feller who tried to shoot you in town," Mose instantly replied. "That feller was little and wore a big cloak. You didn't get a look at his face, boss?"

Slade again shook his head. Leaning against a tree trunk, he rolled a cigarette before speaking again.

"Can you think of anybody that description might fit?"

Mose hesitated. "Boss, the feller I saw last night and the feller you saw tonight kinda fits in with the man I told you about, the one who runs a store."

"You mean Tol Grundy?"

"I ain't sayin' it was Tol Grundy, 'cause I don't know," Mose replied, "but Tol Grundy is a little scrawny feller."

"Lots of little scrawny fellows," Slade commented.

"Uh-huh, that's right," Mose conceded, "but you remember that shotgun you picked up in the alley last night? Remember that gun had a brand new stock? Well, during the ruckus in his store that night, Tol Grundy grabbed up a sawed-off shotgun and a bullet knocked it out of his hands and smashed the stock to smithereens."

Slade nodded. The incident had been included in the sheriff's account of the fight in the store.

"Course there's lots of shotguns, too," Little Mose added, "but strikes me as sort of funny. And I heard those black opal rocks old Cullen grabbed were being sent to Tol Grundy. Maybe Mistuh Grundy's out looking for Cullen. Or do you think he followed us out of town?"

"Not impossible," Slade admitted. "Also not impossible that he was aiming to get ahead of us. If it hadn't been for Mammy Jackson's cat and owl he might have done it.

"Then again he might be anxious to warn somebody we're riding the trail through the Bottoms and to be on the lookout for us. Well, let's go back to Mammy and eat. I gather from what Mammy said there's no riding that trail to the north in the dark."

"Not a chance," Mose replied. "We'll have to stay here with Mammy till it gets light."

When they returned to the cabin, Mammy Jackson had calmly set the table and was heaping plates with fragrant stew. Slade gazed at her in admiration. She interpreted his look and laughed.

"Seen a few shootings in my time," she remarked. "Remember seeing John Tolliver and Sime Hartsook shoot a duel over a gal that wasn't worth fighting for. They plumb missed each other, but a bullet nicked a patch of skin off the end of my nose. Ain't paid much mind to shootings ever since."

"Mammy," Slade chuckled, "you should be with the rangers."

"Suppose you tell your boss-man that," Mammy said.

"And how does she know *that!*" mumbled Little Mose through a mouthful of stew.

Six

SLADE AND MOSE slept in the back room of the cabin. Mose was snoring almost before his head hit the pillow, but Slade lay awake, thinking.

Although he had no proof that the man who tried to drygulch him or the horseman he had glimpsed at the edge of the moon-dappled clearing was Tol Grundy, Slade was inclined to believe that Little Mose was right in his surmise that the two had been the same and that in each case it had been the Dallas storekeeper. If so, the important question to Slade's way of thinking was why should Grundy try to kill him.

According to Sheriff Dawes' account of the affair, Grundy was in the clear so far as the killing was concerned. So why should he be interested in preventing a thorough investigation?

It was not beyond the realm of possibility that something was afoot in which Grundy was implicated, that Grundy was desperately anxious not to have uncovered. Something that a thorough investigation of the Aitken killing probably would uncover, and he was prepared to go to any lengths to balk the investigation.

As to the connection between Grundy and Cullen Baker, he was still vague. And an uneasy premonition was forming in his mind that he was caught in the middle of a falling-out between two outlaw factions. Either that, or Grundy and Baker were working together to double-cross Sabida Quijano.

In either case Slade knew that he personally was in deadly danger. That, however, was nothing new. Just an occupational hazard to which he was accustomed.

He rolled over on his side, seeking sleep.

Outside, the owls whined and hooted. The night wind drew mysterious whispers from the moss-draped trees. The Black Water, running just beyond the clearing, chafed against its black banks.

In the outer room, the great cat padded about on velvet feet, its claws making sibilant little clickings on the floor boards. The white moonlight crept across the clearing and poured a bar of silver radiance through the open window. Little Mose moved restlessly in his sleep and the yellow-eyed owl on the perch rustled its feathers and snapped its hooked beak.

Slade lay wrapped in the eerie spell of the swamplands and when he finally drifted off to sleep it was to dream of witches and warlocks and stark elementals that lived in the rolling balls of fen fire and gibbered to the moon.

It was different the next morning, with the rising sun flooding the clearing with liquid gold and birds singing on the boughs. After a good breakfast Slade and Little Mose set out, riding north through the shadows under the trees.

"If you don't find old Cullen, come back and maybe we can figure something," was Mammy Jackson's parting injunction.

The trail they followed, little more than a game track, wound and twisted between the great tree trunks. Through the interlacing branches above, little sunlight penetrated. They rode for the most part in an eerie green twilight with occasional dapplings of gold where a vagrant beam penetrated the leafy umbrella. To their right flowed the broad sheet of the Black Water, sullen and mysterious, with no ripple to break its oily surface.

"Don't nothing live in there, not even a gator or a snake," Little Mose declared. "That water is plumb pizenous to everything. That is except old Cullen Baker. He swum it, and lived to tell about it."

Slade knew that the somber color of the stream was the result of decaying vegetation and he suspected that once the sun had warmed the water sufficiently there would be plenty of aquatic life apparent.

Little Mose was nervous and ill at ease, casting frequent glances over his shoulder and peering into the semi-gloom ahead.

The afternoon was well along when Mose told Slade that they were but a few miles from the northern edge of the forest.

"Up there is the prairie," he said. "The Brazos Trail runs right by the north end of the woods. Understand that trail runs all the way south to Mexico."

Slade nodded thoughtfully, his black brows drawing together. He felt there was a significance in the proximity of the trail to the swamplands.

"We must be getting close to where that old cabin is," Mose remarked a little later. "I ain't never seen it, but I know pretty well just about where it should be. It's stuck back in the woods on a little cleared patch an old trapper cut out a long time back. He lived there and trapped in the woods. Lots of good pelt critters in the Bottoms.

"It's a plumb bad section, boss, always was and always will be. Almost as bad as the Big Thicket country down to the south that I've heard about."

"Yes, it's as bad as the Big Thicket," Slade agreed. "I've been there. The Big Thicket isn't swampland like this."

"Swampland is the worst of all," said Mose. "In swampland if you don't know the trails you're a goner."

They had covered the better part of a mile, very slowly, through the ever thickening growth when Slade abruptly reined in.

"I smell smoke," he said.

Little Mose sniffed sharply, his wide nostrils flaring. "Me, too," he whispered. "Somebody got a wood fire going up ahead."

"Which means that somebody is in that cabin," Slade said. "Mose, we'd better leave the horses here and cover the rest of the way on foot. That smoke isn't far off."

They concealed the horses in a dense thicket and moved forward, careful not to tread on any dry branch or loose stone. They had covered less than a hundred yards when the growth began to thin somewhat, although it remained dense enough to provide good cover. Finally they reached the last straggle of chaparral. Through a fringe of branches they saw a weatherbeaten cabin sitting in a tiny clearing. The growth walled the clearing solidly on all sides, with a single narrow opening breaking the tangle to the north, where the trail they followed proceeded on its way. To one side of the cabin was a pole lean-to under which stood two horses and more than a dozen smaller, long-eared creatures.

"Pack mules," Slade breathed. "And there are only two horses tethered there with the mules. Which should mean there are only two men in the cabin."

From the stick-and-mud chimney of the cabin rose a thread of blue smoke. A closed door faced the two watchers, and a single dirty-paned window.

Slade studied the cabin in silence. He could make out no sign of life other than the steady smoke trickle.

"Mose," he said at length, "I wonder if that shack has a back door?"

"Most of those old cabins have," Mose replied.

Slade nodded. "You stay here and keep a watch on the front," he said. "I'll be back in a minute."

He slid through the growth silent as an Indian until he had circled the clearing.

The cabin did have a back door, and it stood slightly ajar. Through the opening came the sound of rough

voices and a rattle of tinware. Evidently the occupants
of the cabin were preparing a meal.

He retraced his steps to where the little man waited
and explained to Mose what he had learned.

"Now here's the plan," he said. "Give me plenty of
time to get in back of the cabin again. Then throw down
on the window. Shoot once, no more. Otherwise you
might wing me."

"But what if one of them happens to be Cullen Baker?"
Mose whispered.

"Got to take the chance," Slade replied. "Here we go."

"So long, boss."

Slade reached his former position behind the cabin.
He paused, drew both guns and stood tense and ready.
Slowly the seconds crawled by. Slade began to wonder
uneasily if something had gone wrong. The silence remained unbroken. Talk had ceased inside the cabin, but
the rattle of knives and forks on tin plates continued.
Evidently the men were absorbed by their food.

The crash of Mose's gun made Slade jump a foot. A
clatter and tinkle of broken glass echoed the report, and
a storm of shouts. There was the crash of an overturned
chair, the tinny clang of a platter on the floor, and a thud
of boots.

Slade leaped, hit the sagging door with his shoulder
and crashed it open. Two men, guns in hands, were peering cautiously through the shattered window. They
whirled at the sound of his entrance and gaped squarely
into the black muzzles of his Colts. Slade's voice rang
out.

"Drop those guns!"

He stepped forward as he spoke and his foot came
down squarely on a greasy tin plate that had fallen to
the floor. He slipped, floundered off balance.

The two men moved instantly. The cabin rocked and
shivered to the crash of shots.

Seconds later, one sleeve shot to ribbons, blood streaming down his face from a bullet burn across his left cheekbone, Walt Slade peered through the powder fog at the two figures sprawled motionless on the floor. Mose crashed through the front door.

"Lawdy, boss," he panted. "Is that all of 'em?"

"Reckon it is," Slade answered.

"Boss, you're hurt," chattered Mose, holstering his gun and hurrying forward.

"Just a scratch," Slade replied, swabbing blood from his face with his neckerchief.

He glanced apprehensively around the room, for belatedly had come the thought that he might have made a mistake and the two men were but harmless trappers or hunters occupying the old cabin.

His fears were quickly relieved. Resting against the walls were glistening rows of parallel barrels, like the pipes of an organ, scores of them. Mose's gaze followed Slade's.

"Rifle guns!" he exclaimed. "Enough for an army! And look at them packsacks!"

Slade hurried to open one of the aparejos—rawhide packsacks made to fit snugly around the curving sides of a mule and strap beneath its belly.

"Rifle parts," he told Mose. "Mose, it looks like we've hit paydirt, even if we didn't drop a loop on Cullen Baker. I'm willing to bet money that here's where Tol Grundy comes into the picture. This old cabin is an assembling point for stuff slipped in from all over the country. The authorities have suspected that Grundy might be smuggling arms to Sabida Quijano, but they never have been able to get anything on him. His store has been watched, but nothing ever happened there until the other night. Here's where he gets a load together and slides it south by fast mule train, traveling by night, holing up by day."

"You figure Cullen Baker is working with him, boss?"

"I wish I knew," Slade replied. "Baker is mixed up in the deal somehow, just how I don't know."

Slade was examining the bodies of the two dead outlaws when Mose suddenly uttered an exclamation, "Horses, boss, coming this way!"

Seven

SLADE AND MOSE peered through the shattered window. Slade could plainly hear the muffled beat of hoofs somewhere in the growth to the south. Another moment and seven horsemen filed slowly into the clearing, glancing alertly about. In the lead rode a grotesque-looking figure in a long coat.

"The cunjer-man!" breathed Little Mose.

"Yes, Tol Grundy," Slade whispered back. "He and his bunch have come to fix up this stuff for shipment. Easy, Mose, we've got to slide out the back door. Wait till they head for the shack."

The horsemen had clumped together at the edge of the clearing, conferring in low tones.

They were evidently suspicious of the silent cabin with its broken window. Little Mose was in a state of nervous agitation, but Slade lingered.

Finally the outlaws paced their horses slowly toward the cabin, hands on their guns, tense and vigilant.

"Come on," Slade breathed. "We've got to—"

From the opening in the north wall of the growth bulged another group of horsemen, nearly a dozen. At their head rode a bearded giant with blazing black eyes and a livid scar stretching from the corner of his right eye to his ear.

"Cullen Baker!" Slade breathed.

"Old Cullen himself!" gulped Little Mose.

Cullen Baker uttered a wild yell as he sighted the riders approaching the cabin. Instantly the clearing burst into an inferno of gunfire.

Slade and Little Mose saw stricken men fall, horses

61

rear and plunge. An unmanageable horse bolted, crashing into the growth. The low branches swept the rider from its back to lie motionless at the edge of the clearing.

Yells, curses, howls of pain and the screams of frenzied horses merged with the roar of the guns. The scar-faced Cullen Baker, raging in the van of his men, was shooting with both hands. Slade saw him line sights with Tol Grundy, saw the storekeeper reel in his saddle and fall, writhing on the grass, kicked and trampled to a pulp by the maddened horses.

Grundy's men, outnumbered, had no chance to run. One by one they fell.

As abruptly as it began the fight ended. The grass was strewn with bodies. Riderless horses milled about. Cullen Baker and two of his followers alone remained in their saddles.

Slade stepped back from the window. As Baker and his two men holstered their guns, Slade flung open the cabin door and stepped out, a gun in each hand. His voice rolled across the clearing.

"Elevate! In the name of the State of Texas! You are under arrest!"

Baker and his men jerked like galvanized frogs, glaring and mouthing, then slowly raised their hands shoulder high. Slade's voice rang out again.

"Under the authority of the Texas Rangers—"

Across the clearing a gun blazed. Slade staggered back and fell heavily. With a yell of rage, Mose fired his gun at a man standing at the far edge of the clearing, the outlaw who was swept from his bolting horse by the branches and had lain momentarily stunned by the fall. He went down again, this time to stay down.

The crash of Mose's gun was echoed by Slade's as, prone on the ground, he traded shots with Cullen Baker and his men.

One of the horsemen reeled from his saddle. An instant later the second owlhoot slumped forward and fell like a sack of old clothes. Cullen Baker wheeled his horse and fled for the opening in the growth as Slade's hammers clicked on empty shells. As he vanished, the empty guns dropped from Slade's hands and he slumped forward on his face, breathing in hoarse gasps, his face contorted with pain.

Little Mose ran to Slade and knelt beside him.

"You all right, boss, you all right?" he exclaimed in a voice of agony.

"Got me along the ribs," Slade panted. "I'm paralyzed."

Little Mose tore open his shirt and bared The Hawk's sinewy chest. His voice rose in supreme thanksgiving.

"Now praise the good Lord! Just knocked a hunk of meat off the outside. Hit you a devil of a lick, boss, but she didn't go through. Now you just take it easy while I tie it up."

"Let it bleed a little first," Slade told him. "You go fetch the horses and then I'll let you strap me up. There's a roll of bandage and a little jar of antiseptic salve in the saddle pouch."

"Okay," said Mose as he stuffed fresh cartridges into his gun, "but first I'm going to make sure no more of them devils come to life."

Little Mose examined the bodies strewn around the clearing.

"All done for, boss," he called. Slade lay back on the grass, feeling weak and sick. The glancing blow of a Forty-five slug on a bone is no light matter.

However when Mose returned with the horses he was sitting up. The little man deftly dressed the ugly furrow along his ribs and helped him don his shirt.

"Now what, boss?" he asked.

Slade got to his feet, shakily. "We'll haul those car-casses out of the cabin and see if we can round up some hot coffee and something to eat," he said.

When they entered the cabin, Mose insisted that Slade lie down on one of the bunks built against the walls. His wiry strength was surprising in so small a frame and he hauled the bodies out with no difficulty. Then he got the rigs off the horses and discovered feed under the lean-to. He did the same for the outlaws' mounts that were wandering about the clearing and then turned them loose to graze.

"I turned those mules loose, too," he told Slade when he returned to the cabin. "Reckon they'll hang around this patch where the grass is good."

Slade agreed as he rolled a cigarette and smoked while Mose built up the fire in the stove.

"Plenty of eatings here," Mose announced after an examination of the provisions on the shelves. "Plenty of coffee in the pot, too, and it's beginning to simmer. I'll pour you a cup right off."

They ate by the light of a couple of bracket lamps for it was full dark outside. Mose glanced dubiously at the window but Slade allayed his fears.

"Nobody can get anyways close without Shadow letting us know about it," he explained. "Anyhow, it's highly unlikely if there's any of either bunch, Grundy's or Baker's, left alive. Aside from Baker."

Slade stretched out on one of the bunks and thought things over. Cullen Baker had made good his escape and he had a long start. The question was, where had he gone?

Slade was still uncertain as to just what was back of the row between Baker and Tol Grundy.

Where had Baker gone? That he must learn. But how?

"Figure it's safe to sleep, boss?" Mose asked after he had cleaned up the dishes and the stove.

"Don't think we have anything to worry about. And Shadow will let us know if anybody comes nosing around," Slade decided. "Prop a chair against each door so it'll give us warning if anybody tries to come in, and blow out the lights."

With these matters attended to, Mose lay down and was instantly asleep. Slade himself did not remain awake for long. He was still weak and very weary. His skinned rib had ceased to throb and now the important thing was to rest and get himself back into shape.

He went to sleep.

Eight

THE SUN WAS SHINING brightly when Slade awoke. Mose already had a fire going in the stove and was making preparations for breakfast.

"How you feeling?" he asked.

"My ribs are sore as the devil but otherwise, I'm okay," Slade replied, swinging his feet to the floor. "Soon as I move around and get rid of the stiffness I'll be all set. How are you?"

"If all the haunts in the Bottoms had squalled at once last night they couldn't have woke me up," Mose declared. "You keep an eye on this bacon, and I'll get some water from the spring back of the shed. Reckon a good wash-up in cold water won't hurt either one of us."

After breakfast, Slade examined the bodies of the dead owlhoots.

"What we going to do with 'em?" Mose asked.

"Pack them in the cabin and leave them for the sheriff," Slade decided. "If he wants to ride up and look them over, okay. He might recognize some of them."

"And the guns and the packsacks?"

"We'll take them back with us," Slade said.

Rounding up the mules that were nosing about the clearing was an easy task, but loading the packs and the assembled arms was considerable of a chore. They accomplished it by mid-morning and headed south, arriving at Mammy Jackson's clearing at sunset.

"Yes, old Cullen went past this way, or so I was told," Mammy answered Slade's question. "He went by like he had places to go and his watch was slow."

"Then he's definitely headed for Mexico," Slade said.

66

"Going after him and give him his come-uppance?" Mammy asked.

"I'm going after him, that's sure," Slade answered. "But so far he's been coming out ahead in the deal."

"Won't last," said Mammy. "Good is the rooster that always wins the fight at the last. Yep, when he looks to be dead he gets up again and kicks the devil in the belly and stands on him and crows. You'll get him, Mistuh Slade."

"I hope you're right," Slade said, chuckling at the old woman's metaphor.

"Come on and eat. I got fried chicken and hot biscuits and gravy all ready. Figured you'd be along about now," declared Mammy.

"How'd she figure that when we didn't even know it ourselves," muttered Mose. "And we got to sleep here again with that cunjer owl and that witch cat."

The night passed without incident and in the bright sunshine of the following morning Mose felt better.

"Witches can't work no spells in the daytime," he confided to Slade, "but just the same I'll be glad when we get out of the swamplands."

"We should hit Dallas before dark," Slade predicted as they said goodbye to Mammy Jackson and headed south.

An astonished man was Sheriff Pres Dawes when Slade and Mose rode up to his office with their train of laden mules.

"And Grundy got it, eh?" he remarked after listening to their account of what happened. "I always knew that man was crooked as a snake in a cactus patch, but I could never get anything on him. A shame Baker got away. You going after him, Slade?"

Slade nodded.

"How do you figure to work it?"

Slade pondered before answering. Then he said, "My

hunch is that he plans to tie up with Sabida Quijano, and Quijano is operating along the Border between Brownsville and Laredo. Mostly south of the line. So, I'm going to take a train to Brownsville or Laredo and get to the Border ahead of him."

"You have no authority in Mexico," the sheriff commented.

Slade shrugged. "Granted—as a Texas Ranger."

Looking at his bleak face, Sheriff Dawes was pretty sure that Cullen Baker would never find sanctuary in Mexico or anyplace else.

"You figure to take your horse along, of course," he observed.

"Yes," Slade replied.

"I'll arrange for your transportation," volunteered the sheriff. "I know the division superintendent and he'll fix it up."

"Thanks," Slade nodded. "The sooner the better."

"I'll take care of it right away," promised the sheriff. "I expect you can catch the cannonball that leaves about daylight."

Slade spent the night in Mose Wagner's cabin. The following morning, before he boarded the caboose of the fast freight, he said goodbye to the little man.

"Hope to be seeing you soon again," he said. "I'll never forget the help you gave me. Take care of yourself."

"I'll look after him," promised the sheriff. "I won't even lock him up when he deserves to be. Telling folks that sugar water will cure the mis'ry!"

Slade smiled as he waved goodbye to the little Negro.

It was a long ride from Dallas to the Mexican Border and at the last minute he decided not to stop at Brownsville but go on to Laredo.

Upon arriving at Laredo and securing accommodations for himself and his horse, Slade paid a visit to an official of the United States Customs Office, Laredo being a minor port of entry.

"Quijano!" growled the official when Slade broached the object of his visit. "He's a confounded pest and the smartest smuggler we've ever had to deal with. He's been making us look like a bunch of fumbling school boys."

"Shoving stuff across, eh?" Slade remarked.

"Yes, and getting it shoved across to him. And how we don't know."

"Not difficult to ford the Rio Grande when it's low," Slade observed.

"Granted," retorted the official, "but how about when that infernal river is really high and running 600,000 cubic feet a second past here?"

"Would be considerable of a chore," Slade conceded.

"To that I'll agree," said the Customs man, "but that's when they've been getting the stuff across. Twice when the river was in that condition and utterly unfordable as you know, small Mexican patrols have encountered that blasted smuggling train and fought with them. Both times they were beaten off, but each time by chance they managed to kill a pack mule. Both times the aparejos were crammed with rifle parts and cartridges. And both times those rawhide packsacks were soaking wet and the mules were wet, just as if they had recently swum the river, which was absolutely impossible."

"Didn't rain hard that night?"

"Hadn't been any rain for a week," the official grunted. "You know the Rio Grande doesn't flood from rain down here. What takes place at the headwaters of the Pecos and other streams is what's responsible for flood conditions here."

"Sure those patrols were responsible and could be trusted to tell the truth?" Slade asked.

"No reason to believe otherwise," replied the Customs

man. "But admitting they were a bunch of liars, I'm not inclined to put our own patrols in that category. And as it happens, one of our patrols consisting of three men, had a brush with a train that showed up a little to the north of here. They managed to down a mule with packs loaded with contraband dobe dollars, marihuana and other junk. Well, that mule was wet and so was the pack, and the river running like a Comanche buck full of red-eye."

Slade nodded thoughtfully.

"How about the Indian crossing north of the river end of Bruni Street here in Laredo? The Indians knew it centuries before white men discovered it by chance. Not so many years back the Indians used it to cross cattle and horses rustled from the settlers."

"You mean that ledge of limestone lying just below the surface of the water? Yes, it provides a ford even when the river is fairly high. But when the river is really in flood, I doubt if even a very good and very strong horse with a skillful rider could make it, certainly not loaded mules. In fact, I don't think anything could cross it then. Would be even more dangerous than trying to swim the river above or below it. The current would sweep a horse or a mule right off the ledge and the whirlpools formed by the obstruction would suck it under instantly. No, that isn't worth considering during really high water. Just the same, though, we have it guarded and the Mexicans guard it on their side. Those pack mules certainly didn't cross there."

Slade nodded again and for a moment was silent.

"Any chance for, say, a single horseman to slip past the patrols and get across?" he asked casually.

"Possibly on a dark night, although he'd be taking a chance," the official admitted. "But certainly not a troop and a train of mules. That would be completely out of the question."

"And you think Quijano heads the smuggling bunch?"

"Oh, there's little doubt as to that," the Customs man replied. "In fact he brags about it, how he makes fools of the patrols. And the hellion's got a right to brag," he added with a wry smile. "If he wasn't such a pest and such an all around ruthless devil, you'd have to admire the scoundrel for the way he puts it over. But—" and the official's face hardened, "the sidewinders killed one of our men less than a month ago, and we're not seeing anything admirable about that."

"Mind giving me the details?" Slade asked.

"Not at all," said the other. "It happened just north of the ruins of an old Mission House that sits on a rise close to the north bank of the river. He'd been shot twice through the body and through the head. Some cowhands from a ranch farther north found him and didn't have any difficulty reconstructing what had happened. They found where he had ridden down from the north, where his horse began cutting capers when the shooting started. Then they found where the bunch he had the run-in with came riding up from the south. The ground was soft along there and of course it wasn't hard for experienced plainsmen to read the signs. They said there must have been thirty or forty critters altogether and there were plenty of mule prints along with the tracks left by the horses. They said the mule prints were deep, showing that they were loaded heavily. They figured it was a pack train of better than twenty mules with a dozen or more riders along with them. Nobody but Quijano could have been running an outfit that large. So you see us fellows haven't much reason to love him."

"Yes, I see," Slade said quietly. "Just where in relation to town is the spot where the fight occurred?"

"About five miles to the west of Laredo and a quarter of a mile or so west of the trail that runs to the north."

"Which makes it appear they didn't cross by way of the ford we were discussing," Slade commented.

"They certainly didn't," replied the Customs man.

"And what shape was the river in that night?"

"High, higher even than it is right now."

"Which would cause one to assume that they couldn't possibly have forded the Rio Grande with a train at that point."

"Not unless the critters sprouted wings," grunted the official.

"Which is rather unlikely," Slade smiled. "And which brings us right back to where we started. Somehow, Quijano runs stuff back and forth across the river no matter in what condition it is."

"That's right," the Customs man admitted. "The Mexican authorities are plumb frantic, because they know Quijano is getting arms and ammunition across and they're afraid he'll start a half-baked revolution. However, I don't think they have anything to worry about on that score. Quijano isn't interested in 'freeing' the peons. He's an outlaw pure and simple and has no ambition to be otherwise."

"But he has a numerous following," Slade remarked.

"He sure has," conceded the official, "and if he keeps getting guns and ammunition like he has of late he'll soon be in a position to outfit a small army."

"And suppose," Slade said, "that an abler and more ambitious man should depose Quijano, take over his following and set up as a liberator with the object of establishing an outlaw empire which would encompass all the north of Mexico?"

"Then," the official replied grimly, "there would be real trouble along the Border and you fellows would have your hands full. What makes you ask such a question?"

"Because," Slade said quietly, "that's just what's liable to happen."

The Customs man stared. "You really believe that's possible?" he asked.

"That's my opinion," Slade answered.

"But who?" demanded the official.

"Ever hear of Cullen Baker?"

"Of course, who hasn't?" the other replied. "But I thought the rangers killed Baker up on the Red River."

"That's what the rangers thought, too," Slade answered dryly. "However, it seems the report of Cullen Baker's death was greatly exaggerated. He's very much alive and he's headed this way if he hasn't already arrived, although I don't think he has just yet."

The Customs man whistled. "Now you *have* got me worried," he said. "What are you going to do about it?"

"I'm going to try and drop a loop on Baker," Slade replied. "I hope to be able to reach him through Quijano. Tell me, just what do you know about Quijano?"

"Not a great deal," the other admitted. "He's a daring rogue with the disposition of a tail-scorched Gila Monster when he's aroused. I understand he has the best blood of Spain in his veins and that his grandmother was a Yaqui princess, which gives him, in addition, the cunning and ferocity of the mountain Indians."

Slade nodded. He was familiar with the type and was not particularly impressed.

"What does he look like?" he asked.

"The descriptions I've been able to get are conflicting and confusing. Some say he has black whiskers, others say they're red, still others say he hasn't any whiskers. I've heard men who claim to have seen him swear he's got a big scar on his face, while others declare he hasn't any scar. In my opinion he's mighty good at disguises."

"Scars can be faked with grease paint, and false

whiskers can be changed," Slade commented. "Anything else?"

"About the only thing agreed on is he's big and tall," said the official.

"Know anything concerning his habits—what he does for recreation, where he shows up, his tastes?"

"He is undoubtedly a man of some education—Mission schooled, I'd say. They say he reads, drinks sparingly, isn't a fool over women, though he likes them, plays cards occasionally and is very fond of good music."

"How's that?" Slade asked quickly. "Fond of music?"

"So I've been told," the official replied. "I've heard that sometimes he will take over one of the *cantinas* in Nuevo Laredo across the river and have the orchestra —they've got some good ones over there—play all evening for him and then give the leader a double-handful of gold pieces."

"He shows up in Nuevo Laredo, then?"

"Oh, sure! You know how it is the other side of the river—grease the right palms and everything is okay."

Slade said, "I guess I'll have to get in touch with *Señor* Quijano."

The Customs man looked startled. "Good Lord!" he exclaimed. "I'd as soon get in touch with the Devil! Where do you figure to contact him?"

"In Nuevo Laredo."

"You wouldn't have a chance," the other declared. "You'd be spotted the minute you crossed the bridge."

"I guess you're right about that," Slade conceded. For several moments he sat silent, listening to the howl of the wind and gazing at the rain beating against the window panes that were already darkening with the shades of evening.

"So I won't cross by way of the bridge," he added. "Now I want you to do something for me. I want you to pull your patrol away from the north end of that limestone ford tonight."

This time the Customs man really did stare. "Man, you're crazy!" he sputtered. "You can never do it. You'll just end up getting yourself drowned. And even if you did make it across by some miracle, the Mexican patrol at the south end of the ford would down you for sure. They're trigger happy over there and shoot first and ask questions afterward."

"I reckon I'll risk it," Slade returned. "It promises to be a bad night and they're pretty apt to be staying under cover."

"I still think it's an utterly loco notion," the official protested, shaking his head. "But there's no stopping you fellows when you set your heads to something, no matter how crazy it is. Okay, I'll pull the patrol off. No need for them to be out there in the rain, anyhow."

Slade chuckled and stood up.

"Don't worry," he said. "I'm sure I'll make out okay. And over across there is an old fellow I used to know, and the chances are he's still there. He'll lend me a hand. See you when I come back."

"I'm not going to sit up nights waiting," grunted the Customs man.

Slade laughed again and left the office.

Nine

THE RIO GRANDE was rising. A river of jet under a sky of ebony, it chafed against its banks, quivering the sodden air with a low moaning sound that drifted eerily through the darkness, like the plaint of a monster in pain. Spatters of icy rain struck phosphorescent gleams from the troubled surface as the drops speared downward. High in the sky a cold wind wailed, died to a whisper, wailed again. From shore to shore a tossing ripple surged and undulated where the current pounded against the limestone wall of the Indian crossing. From the north bank, the lights of Nuevo Laredo on the south bank gleamed like mist-washed sparks struggling to survive.

From the dark river emanated a wan, ghostly glow. The faint radiance outlined the form of the great black horse that appeared to be walking on the water.

"Steady, Shadow," Slade cautioned him. "If you slide off this rock we'll both be goners. The river's running like a mill race and rising by the second. Steady! Take your time."

Shadow stepped along, raising his hoofs daintily, making sure of his footing. The water came more than halfway up his iron-hard legs and the push of the current was strong swirling over the limestone ledge. One slip and the whirlpools that raged against the rock barrier would instantly suck them under. And no swimmer could hope to survive in that maelstrom.

Slade strained his eyes toward the distant lights that marked the site of Nuevo Laredo on the Mexican side of the river. He listened intently for any sound that might rise above the moan and mutter of the flooding stream.

As the lights drew nearer he tensed in the saddle. Shadow blew softly through his nostrils. The strengthening push of the rising water was making him nervous. He sensed the danger that lurked in the swirling black depths.

But Slade knew that the threat of the turbulent river was not the only danger they faced.

"Take it easy, now," he whispered to Shadow, "take it easy."

Slowly the winking lights grew larger. Slade could make out the bulk of the town to the south and slightly to the east, a cluster of shadows outlined by the golden necklace of the lights. In a moment would come the test.

If the Mexican patrol was awake and on the job, he had scant chance of remaining undetected after leaving the water. He could feel his palms sweating and his nerves were tight to the breaking point.

But the darkness ahead remained unbroken by sound or movement. The water began to shallow, the ledge became veined and cracked. Shadow stumbled, recovered his balance with an effort and snorted.

"Easy, feller, easy!" Slade cautioned in a whisper. He strained his ears but still could hear no sound other than the moaning cry of the river. A moment later Shadow planted his irons on solid ground and Slade heaved a sigh of relief.

Out of the darkness ahead rang a voice, harsh, commanding.

"*Alto!*" (Halt!) The command was emphasized by the ominous double click of a cocking rifle hammer.

Slade touched Shadow's neck with the rein. "Trail feller, trail!"

Instantly the big black veered sharply to the right and shot forward, his irons drumming the hard soil. There was a spurt of flame, the metallic clang of a rifle. Slade heard the bullet go past. He bent low in the saddle and urged the horse to greater speed. The rifle bloomed again and Slade swore under his breath. He couldn't very well return the fire, the gunman was a Mexican peace officer performing the duty required of him. He bent still lower in the saddle, whispering urgently to Shadow.

The great black responded gallantly. His steely legs worked like pistons, he flattened his ears, slugged his head above the bit and fairly poured his long body over the ground. Behind, the rifle cracked viciously. Something like an urgent finger twitched at Slade's sleeve. Another report, much farther behind now, and his broad-brimmed hat moved slightly on his head.

The rifle blazed once more, but this time Slade did not even hear the bullet. Another moment and they swerved behind a bristle of thicket and were out of range.

Well to the south of the cluster of adobes and other buildings he slowed Shadow's pace and pulled the black to a halt. A small cabin with a stable directly in the rear showed dimly in the faint light filtering through the cloud bank.

Dismounting, he approached the little house with Shadow pacing behind him, and rapped on the door. In a moment there was a sound of shuffling feet. The door opened and an old man appeared, peering with squinted eyes at his visitor. Then recognition wreathed his wrinkled features in a smile.

"*Capitan!*" he exclaimed. "This is indeed a rare sight for my old eyes! Enter! Enter! But stay, there is the *caballo*, who doubtless will also appreciate food and shelter."

He pattered out past Slade and reached a fearless hand to Shadow. The big black snorted, drew back, then stretched forward a friendly nose.

"Ah, he remembers me," said the old Mexican. "Enter, *Capitan*, I will care for him at once, then I will join you."

He led the horse toward the stable in the rear. Slade entered the cabin, bowing his tall head so that his hat crown would not strike against the upper door beam. He closed the door behind him, drew a comfortable chair to the fire that snapped and crackled in the big stone fireplace and sat down, stretching his long legs to the blaze. He was smoking with obvious relish when the old Mexican appeared. In a few minutes a fire was going in the stove of the tiny kitchen, coffee was steaming, a pot bubbling on the fireplace knob and the oddly mated pair sat down to an appetizing meal.

The old Mexican asked no questions, but after their hunger was assuaged, he glanced inquiringly at his tall guest.

Slade smoked in silence for several minutes, then abruptly asked a question.

"Felipe," he said, "what do you know about Sabida Quijano?"

The old man stiffened in his chair and peered at Slade, his eyes narrowing slightly.

"Little that is good," he replied. "He is a doer of evil deeds who causes stupid men to think he is great. He is a giant of a man whose strength, it is said, is the strength of six. Certainly he has the sins of six on his soul. He can lift a horse. He can crack a horseshoe with his great hands."

"I've done that myself," Slade interpolated. "It's largely a trick."

"*Si*," the Mexican agreed, "a trick that can be mastered only by one with hands of steel. Sabida Quijano is such a one. Also he is a master with gun and knife. He knows not fear and although he is not normally a cruel man, I would say, in the hour of his anger he knows no mercy. He has been known to bind naked men across ant hills and smear them with honey so that they were eaten alive by the ants. He has crucified others upon the spines of cactuses to die in agony under the burning sun. Why do you ask of him, *Capitan?*"

"I want to see him," Slade replied.

Felipe Montez stared even as the Customs man did. "*Capitan*, Quijano has small use for gringos," he replied. "Arouse his anger and he will do to you even as I just told you he has done to others."

"I'll risk it," Slade said. "Any notion where I can find him? I've heard he shows up in Nuevo Laredo now and then."

"That is so," Felipe admitted. "He is seen here. But, *Capitan*, you could not enter where he goes and hope to intercept him. Not even El Halcon can do that, for El Halcon after all is a gringo, and of all such Quijano is vastly suspicious. He would be warned of your coming and would vanish away. Or, more likely, he would lay a trap for you and, I repeat, to be caught in Sabida Quijano's snare when he is in wrath is to die, horribly."

"Yes," Slade agreed, "but a coyote in a sheep's skin might mingle with the sheep, until they smelled him. And I've a notion Quijano's nose isn't a sheep's nose."

"Be not too sure," cautioned Felipe. "There's a good chance he would smell you out. But if you could appear quite different from what you are, it might work. But how?"

Slade smoked thoughtfully for a moment. "The wandering *trovadors* (troubadors) still sing on the street corners in Nuevo Laredo, do they not?" he asked.

Felipe's black eyes snapped. "They do," he replied.

"Well," Slade observed, "I can sing a little, and I can speak the language. I've heard that Sabida Quijano loves music."

"That is so, *Capitan*," Felipe exclaimed, with considerable more animation of manner. "It is one of his great and strange passions. And with a voice such as yours! *Caspita!*"

"I've a notion it's worth trying," Slade said.

"*Capitan*, if he hears of your voice he will be sure to request that you sing for him," Felipe declared.

"Yes, it's worth trying," Slade repeated. "And first off I want to tell you, Felipe, I am not after Quijano. I'm after a man I feel sure will sooner or later contact him. I hope to get in touch with that man through Quijano."

"I see," nodded Felipe. "Yes, as you say, it is worth trying. I am sure you will be able to approach Quijano through your singing, but pray to the saints he does not suspect you of being other than what you pretend to be. If he does, then we die."

"We?"

"Of course, *Capitan*, I go with you. I will be needed to collect the coins that will shower upon you when you sing," he added with a chuckle. "All *trovadors* are accompanied by a *muchacho* or an old man to collect the coins."

"You will be taking a chance," Slade pointed out.

"*Si*," Felipe admitted composedly. "And how often has El Halcon taken a chance to befriend the lowly? It will be the great pleasure and I will be honored to walk in the shadow of El Halcon."

"Thank you, Felipe," Slade said simply, his eyes all kindness. "Now about a suitable costume. I suppose you can contrive one?"

"That will be simple," said Felipe. "All that is needed are a few pesos spent in the right places, and I have a guitar, as you know. But your skin, *Capitan*? You are burned dark by the sun and the wind, but it is a darkness different from that of the men of *Mejico*."

"I thought of that before I came over," Slade answered. "I brought something with me, something an old Karankawa Indian showed me how to make. The Kranks were the poison-and-herb people of the Texas Indians and were skilled in various concoctions of a lethal and medicinal nature. What I have is a simple dye made from plant roots; their medicine men used it in tribal ceremonies. Rub it on your skin and it will give you just about any shade you want. Plain water doesn't affect it, either. Takes soap, and plenty of it, to get the color off. I've a bottle in my saddle pouch that I mixed up."

"Then there should be little difficulty in gaining entrance to the various *cantinas* and passing as a *trovador* of *Mejico*," said Felipe. "But I fear Sabida Quijano, he has eyes that see all things. He is a hard one to fool, *Capitan*."

"I don't doubt that, but I'm more concerned over the chance that the man I'm looking for won't be fooled. Do you think you can rustle up the clothes I'll need, tonight? If so, I'll get to work with the dye."

"Assuredly," Felipe said. "It is not late and I believe the rain has stopped. I will go at once."

Ten

WITH PLENTY OF MONEY in his pocket, provided by Slade, Felipe left the cabin. Slade got to work with the dye and before Felipe returned the chore was finished. Hands, arms, neck and face showed the coppery tint of the Mexican with much *Indio* blood in his veins. His gray eyes were not particularly noticeable because of the blackness of his thick lashes, and the Spanish blood often accounted for lighter colored eyes in an otherwise dark Mexican. Slade was satisfied.

So was Felipe.

"Verily, I would not know you myself," he declared. "And see, I have the complete costume of the *trovador*."

Slade donned tight-fitting pantaloons, low-cut vest and flowing cloak of green velvet. Down the front of both the cloak and pantaloons were broad yellow stripes on which were embroidered roses, tulips and pansies, life-sized and of brilliant color. Snowy white shirt, black tie, flat velvet cap and fancily stitched boots completed the costume. The guitar Felipe produced was a battered old instrument that nevertheless fretted truly and had a mellow tone. It hung from Slade's shoulder by a faded yellow ribbon.

"Perfect!" exclaimed Felipe.

"Looks sort of like a rainbow that got tangled in a flower garden, but I reckon it'll do," Slade chuckled. Snugged in a shoulder holster under the tight-fitting jacket was a short-barreled Forty-five.

"All right for close work, but uncertain at a distance," he told Felipe. "But it's for certain I can't pack those nine-inch barrels along with me. Well, shall we hit the town tonight and do a little browsing around? It isn't very late."

"Assuredly," said Felipe. "Nuevo Laredo never sleeps."

Together they left the house and when they reached the well-lighted market place, Slade began to strum the guitar and sing. Very quickly a crowd gathered, attracted by the magnificent voice of the tall singer and the masterly manner in which he played the guitar. Felipe, hat in hand, collected the shower of small coins that greeted the completion of each number.

Slade sang only the folk songs of old Mexico, and Spanish ballads, of which he knew many. His Spanish was good enough to pass muster and his costume was no different from that affected by many of the itinerant street musicians.

They moved about and several times were requested to enter *cantinas* and render a number. They were forced to practice a strict moderation or they would soon have been roaring drunk on free wine. It was very late when they returned to the cabin.

"*Capitan*, you would do well to take up street singing as a profession," Felipe chuckled as he emptied his pockets. "Soon you would be rich."

"Maybe you have something there," Slade smiled, "but I'm afraid folks would soon grow tired of me."

"Never!" Felipe declared with conviction.

They continued their nightly performance. The tall troubador with the black hair and sunny eyes became well known in the streets of Nuevo Laredo and his appearance always aroused enthusiasm. And each day Felipe endeavored to pick up information relative to Sabida Quijano, and learned nothing.

"But soon he will appear, *Capitan*, never fear," the old Mexican declared.

However it was not until the seventh day that Felipe came hurrying in as twilight was falling.

"*Capitan*, he is here!" he said. "And I have learned where he will drink wine and listen to music this night. He has many men with him who will mingle with the people in the street and sit at tables in the *cantina*. Do you dare risk it, *Capitan?*"

"Guess so," Slade replied cheerfully. "This is what we've been tramping the streets for."

After singing for a while in the market place, Felipe led the way along a street to where it curved and ran parallel to the waterfront. Here were small *cantinas* with softly shaded lights, from which came the sound of music and laughter and the clinking of bottles on glass. More than once they received invitations to enter, but at a muttered word from old Felipe, Slade each time smilingly declined. Finally they came opposite a rather larger establishment. Here the lights were even dimmer. From the interior came a hum of talk and the soft music of several muted instruments. Felipe uttered a low exclamation.

"He is within, *Capitan*," he whispered. "That is his song they are playing—'*Luz de las Estrellas!*' "

" 'Starlight,' " Slade translated. "I know that one, Felipe."

"Sing it, *Capitan*, sing it!" the Mexican urged. "It will assuredly gain us entrance."

Slade, sweeping a crashing chord from the guitar, pealed forth his baritone-bass in the words of the beautiful Spanish love song.

> Softly the night of stars and a mellow moon
> Sleeps 'neath a robe of shadows,
> And comes the dawn, too soon!

Inside the *cantina* there was a sudden hush, then the sobbing strings of the instruments stilled. Bottles and glasses ceased to clink. Before the second stanza of the song was finished, the portly *cantina* owner was outside the door. He bowed to Slade, held up his hand. Slade stopped singing and muted the strings of his guitar.

"*Señor*," said the *posadero*, "there is within a *caballero* who requests that you enter and sing for him, a *caballero* most generous. It would be well for you to enter, *señor*."

"*Gracias*," Slade replied, bowing in turn. "It will be a pleasure."

The *posadero* ushered them into the *cantina*, which was large and comfortably furnished. He led the way to a table where four men were seated.

"The *trovador*, *caballeros*," he said with a low bow.

One of the table's occupants rose to his feet in greeting and Slade looked into the face of a man as tall, almost, as himself and even broader of shoulder and deeper of chest.

It was an arresting face, powerful, large-featured. The firm, compressed mouth was shaded by a thick, close-cropped mustache. The swarthy cheeks were clean-shaven as was the square chin save for a small tuft of beard. The eyes were large and dark and frank looking, but with a sinister expression in the corners of them. The hair, thick and intensely black, was worn long and cut in a square bang across the forehead, Yaqui fashion. A white scar crossed the forehead just below the hairline. Slade did not need to be told that he looked into the face of Sabida Quijano.

Quijano spoke, his voice deep, sonorous. "*Señor*, you will sing for me."

It was a command spoken in a voice accustomed to giving commands and having them obeyed.

Slade sang "Starlight" for him, sang it through the last haunting stanza and the exquisite refrain.

> Lips rose-tinted breathe a story,
> Sweetest story tongue can tell,
> Eyes that pale the stars bright glory
> Speak their sad but fond farewell.

Sabida Quijano listened, his face rapt, eyes dream-filled. Then he clapped his huge hands vigorously and demanded another.

Slade sang for him, song after song, and meanwhile studied and estimated the bandit leader. An able man, he deduced, but with a mind not overly alert and, perhaps, inclined to indolence. Just another brush-popping outlaw of better than average ability, Slade decided. Plenty of guts, plenty of energy when he cared to exert himself, doubtless a ruthless devil when aroused, but nothing to cause unusual concern along the Border. Sooner or later he would be taken care of.

As Slade sat sipping a glass of wine, a little apart from Quijano's table, the *cantina* doors banged open and a man entered. He glanced about and strode across the room to Quijano's table. He was a giant of a man with hot, glittering black eyes, stretching from the corner of one of which was a long scar. His clothes were powdered with dust and travel-stained. On his cheeks was a two-weeks' growth of black beard.

Cullen Baker!

Sabida Quijano was on his feet, waving a greeting. "*Amigo!* you have returned!" he exclaimed in very good English.

"Yes, I've returned," Baker replied, dropping to the chair that was hurriedly brought for him. Quijano poured him a glass of wine which he downed at a gulp.

He wiped his lips with the back of his hand, glanced around the room. Then he leaned close and began talking to Quijano in a low voice. Slade's keen ears were able to catch only disconnected fragments of the conversation—"Grundy—traitor—aimed to steal—dead."

Quijano's face grew grim as Baker unfolded the story of the fight in the clearing and what led up to it and Tol Grundy's death. At least Slade judged that was what he was relating. Quijano's great hands clenched into trembling fists and he swore a Spanish oath. Then Cullen Baker abruptly drew a small, tightly wrapped package from his pocket and with a few words Slade couldn't catch passed it to Quijano whose face suddenly brightened.

There was no doubt in Walt Slade's mind as to what the package contained, and he was forced to admit admiration for the wily scoundrel's sagacity. How better to convince the bandit leader of his loyalty than to return to him the package of black opals, worth a small fortune? With, doubtless, a convincing yarn of how he, Baker, thwarted Tol Grundy's attempt to double-cross Quijano and steal the gems.

"*Gracias!*" Quijano exclaimed, raising his voice. "*Gracias!* You are a true *amigo!*"

Cullen Baker nodded, but Slade, as his gaze rested on Quijano's face, had a feeling that he was looking at a man already dead.

Before Baker entered the room, Sabida Quijano had been the focus at the table. Slade was struck by the fact that now Cullen Baker dominated the group while apparently deferring to Quijano. The man's fierce and restless energy showed in every line of his ruthless face and vigorous body. Cullen Baker was something to reckon with.

Quijano abruptly remembered his troubador. He

beckoned Slade. "You will sing for my *amigo, si?*" he said.

Slade smiled and nodded. As he played a prelude, Cullen Baker's hot glance swept over his face and form, indifferently. His gaze dropped to the slender, powerful hands that held the guitar and fixed there, fascinated apparently by the deft grace of the slim, dark fingers caressing the strings.

Slade experienced a sudden sense of uneasiness. What did the keen-eyed devil see that interested him so? A moment later Baker's gaze shifted and he appeared to take no further interest in the musician.

Quijano smiled warmly when the song finished with a crash of chords. Again he clapped his hands in unreserved applause.

Slade sang other songs, *La Paloma;* the beautiful *Via Sola* (The Lonely Road). Finally Quijano rose to his feet. His eyes rested on The Hawk's face and tall form. He appeared to be satisfied with what he saw, for he nodded approvingly.

"I must go," he said. "*Señor*, you will come again tomorrow night. *Si? Adios*, then, till tomorrow night." He dropped several gold pieces into Felipe's hand and strode out. Cullen Baker sauntered after him without a glance at Slade. Immediately other men got up from various tables and left the room.

"None but his men will be permitted to leave at once," Felipe breathed to Slade. "It would be well for you to sing another number before we leave."

Slade nodded agreement and proceeded to do so. Shortly afterward Slade and Felipe left the place and headed for home. As they passed between a straggle of dark houses, neither saw the sinister shadows trailing them on either side. Their first warning was a rush of feet from the darkness.

Slade's hand streaked to his gun, but the attackers were upon him. He grappled with one man and hurled him sideways over his shoulder. His fist swept a second to the ground. Another slashing blow to the mouth brought a cry of pain from a third. Then a gun barrel crunched against his head and a wave of blackness swept over him.

Eleven

WHEN WALT SLADE regained consciousness he was dimly aware of a jerking, swaying motion, a prodigious ache in his head and an equally intolerable ache to his back and shoulder muscles. Gradually he realized that he was mounted on a horse, slumped forward in the saddle, his face buried in the animal's coarse mane. His hands were securely bound behind his back, his ankles lashed to the stirrup straps, and the feel of the cords told him they were hair rope, practically unbreakable.

Although his strained muscles cried out for relief from his cramped position, he remained slumped forward listening intently.

He heard no sound save an occasional grunt and the babbling voice of Felipe calling on the saints. A hot anger at himself seethed in his breast. He had been beautifully outsmarted. Cullen Baker had caught on, and Slade was beginning to understand how. Not that it mattered. Baker *had* caught on, that was enough.

For some time the group of horses forged ahead, then abruptly came to a halt. Slade groaned, retched, simulated returning consciousness. He straightened in the saddle, rejoicing at the relief the altered position gave him. He could hear their captors dismounting. Their shapes were but shadows in the darkness and Slade could just make out the dim bulk of a low hill rising directly ahead. Another moment and his ankles were loosed, he was hauled from the saddle and thrown to the ground.

He offered no resistance as his ankles were bound tightly together and he was lifted to the shoulders of four men who walked forward with him. Another moment and their footsteps echoed hollowly. Slade could hear a gurgle of running water and was abruptly aware that he was burning with thirst.

A light flared up, another and another. The blazing torches showed Slade that his bearers were trudging along a narrow tunnel or corridor. Moldy beams, ponderous and square, ribbed the rock walls, with transverse timbers spanning the uprights. To one side ran a small but steady stream of water.

For a considerable distance the silent bearers followed the damp tunnel, then abruptly turned into a side corridor, pausing eventually before a stout wooden door which one swung open. The torchlight revealed a square, rock-walled chamber.

Slade was dropped to the rock floor, and Felipe was dumped beside him. Gazing upward he got his first look at his captors. They were pure-blood Yaqui Indians with dark, impassive faces, save one whose lips were puffed and bloody, who glared murder at The Hawk. Slade reasoned that the blow of his fist had relieved him of a few front teeth.

Not a word was spoken. The group turned, walked out the door and slammed it shut behind them. Blackness blanketed the rocky chamber. Slade heard no click of turning key or rattle of shot bolt. No reason for locking the door. The captives, securely trussed up, would remain right where they were.

Felipe began to scream. "*Sangre de Cristi!*" he howled. "We will die in the dark! We will starve and the rats will gnaw our bones. *Madre de Dios,* intercede for us. Saint Cristofer, aid me!"

Raucous laughter beyond the closed door, fading away, echoed his frenzied supplications, the first sound uttered by the Yaquis.

"Take it easy, fellow, take it easy!" Slade cautioned.

Felipe continued to howl and scream. Slade felt an icy cold settling about his heart. There was grim truth in what the old Mexican shrieked. Doubtless they *would* starve and die in the dark. Their chances to escape were practically nil. The Yaquis knew their business when it came to trussing up a prisoner. The man didn't live who could cut a hair rope with his teeth. That required a knife, and a sharp one.

The old man kept yelling and crying, howling prayers to the saints. Then abruptly he ceased.

"I judge they should be out of hearing by now, *Capitan*," he said in perfectly normal tones.

Slade tried to stare at him through the black dark. "Why the act?" he asked.

"Let them truly believe that we despair," Felipe answered. "Otherwise they might wonder, and perhaps return to search our persons with greater thoroughness, and discover what in their haste they overlooked."

"What's that?" Slade asked eagerly.

"My knife," said Felipe. "It is a small knife but very sharp. It lies in a sheath between my shoulder blades. They felt the back of my neck but did not feel quite low enough."

"I'll have to tear your shirt off with my teeth. Turn onto your side, and I'll start work. And keep on talking, that's the only way I can locate you in this infernal dark," Slade said.

"May the saints aid you!" Felipe prayed. He added grimly, "It was not altogether an act when I called on them for succor. I know this place. It is an old mine, abandoned for many years, miles to the west of town. Nobody ever comes here for it is said to be haunted. Sincerely I called on the blessed ones for aid. Here man is of no avail."

Clumsily, Slade rolled and writhed until his body was against Felipe's. After several futile attempts he managed to get the Mexican's shirt collar between his teeth. But as he tugged and hauled and wrenched, he quickly realized what a monumental task he had set himself. The tough fabric resisted his efforts and Slade cursed the needle work that sewed the garment so firmly. His muscles aching with strain, sweat pouring from every pore, a new terror suddenly intruded. Perhaps Baker and Quijano had no intention of leaving their prisoners to starve peacefully. Perhaps they had other notions as to how they should die and would shortly appear to put their intentions into practice. The time element abruptly looked gigantic and threatening.

After what seemed an eternity of futile tugging and hauling, the shirt tore down the back. Frantically Slade nuzzled and groped till he got the haft of the little knife between his teeth and managed to draw it from the sheath. He inched his body over the rock floor and at last set the blade against the cords that bound Felipe's wrists.

But he quickly realized he could not cut them while holding the knife by the handle. With only his neck muscles to work with, he couldn't exert enough force against the tough hair rope. With a muttered oath, he flopped over on his face and let the knife tinkle to the ground. After more tedious and laborious groping he got the blade between his teeth, writhed back into position and again started sawing on the cords. Instantly he felt the sting of the steel lacerating his lips. Soon his mouth was full of blood. Felipe winced and Slade knew the knife point was nicking the flesh of his wrists. But the old man uttered only words of encouragement.

"You are doing it, *Capitan*, you are succeeding," he declared. "I can feel the strands sever and loosen. Just a little more!"

Every muscle in Slade's body was a fiery agony. His neck throbbed and ached, his throat was constricted. The taste of blood in his mouth was nauseating, red flashes stormed before his eyes and his lungs labored till they threatened to burst his chest. His heart fluttered and its spasmodic beat seemed like thunder in the silence.

With the convulsive energy of despair, he hooked the

knife blade under the cords, his teeth clenched on the
steel, and surged backward with all of his swiftly ebbing
strength.

The hair rope resisted, gave, and then the keen steel
won its victory. Slade fell over backward as the blade
slid through the last strand. Felipe uttered a heartfelt
prayer of gratitude to the saints.

"Just a moment, *Capitan!*" he exclaimed, "till I rub
some feeling into my wrists. There, that is better. The
knife, I must find the knife!"

Slade felt the fumbling hands pass over his face, scratch
and scrabble on the stone. Felipe ejaculated triumph.
Another moment and he was sawing at the rope that
bound Slade's wrists.

"Now your ankles," he said as the cords fell away.
"Then I will loosen my own."

Another instant and both were free. Slade chafed his
wrists, kicked with his feet and finally managed to
stagger erect. He reached down a groping hand and
helped Felipe to rise.

"Able to make it now?" he asked. "Fine! let's get out
of here in case those devils take a notion to come back.
Thank the Lord they didn't fasten the door shut."

They groped their way to the door, shoved it open on
creaking hinges and staggered down the tunnel. The
sound of the little stream told them when they reached
the main corridor and the direction of its flow showed
them which way to turn. A few minutes later they saw
light ahead and quickly gained the outer world.

As soon as his dazzled eyes adjusted themselves to the
light, Slade glanced about apprehensively. In all direc-
tions the terrain appeared devoid of life. To the east a
distant smudge against the blue of the sky denoted the
site of Nuevo Laredo although the town itself was invisible. To the left, no great distance off, flowed the Rio
Grande and beyond the far bank on a slight rise, was a

picturesque ruin that he knew must be the old Mission House near which the Customs agent was killed. He turned and gave attention to his immediate surroundings. They stood at the base of a long low hill that rose south of the river bank. In its flank was the dark tunnel mouth of the ancient mine. Where they stood was considerably lower than the river bank, so that it looked as if the Rio Grande flowed above them.

"I've a notion that in times of flood, all this lowland is under water," he remarked to Felipe. "Well, that looks like a trail over there to the south; we might as well make for it and head for home."

"How are your wrists?" Slade asked as they started walking.

"Just a few small cuts, nothing to speak of," replied the Mexican. "But your lips, *Capitan*, they are lacerated."

"Just scratches," Slade said. "I'd have been willing to saw off an ear or two to get out of there."

The ground over which they passed was hard and stony, but about halfway to the trail there was a stretch of softer strata. As they crossed it, Slade halted, staring at the ground. In the surface were scored a number of prints.

"Horses, a lot more than came here with us last night. And mule prints, too. Now what the devil does this mean?"

He studied the multitude of hoof marks. "Several days' old," he observed. "Most of them, at any rate, including these made by the mules."

He turned and stared back the way they had come. "Felipe," he said, "I'm darned if it doesn't look like Quijano's smuggling train came this way. But how the devil could they get across the river if they did?"

Again he examined the prints. "Here are a few fresher tracks, made last night, some pointing north, some south, but all the others point north. Not long ago a troop of horses and mules passed this way going north, presumably to the Rio Grande. Could there possibly be another ford somewhere hereabouts, a wider and easier-to-cross ledge than the one at Nuevo Laredo?"

"I never heard of such a thing, and I was born and brought up here," Felipe answered. "And surely such a crossing would be revealed in times when the river is low."

"It would sure seem that way," Slade was forced to admit. "But if those horses and mules weren't headed for the river, where were they headed for?"

"Perhaps the *bandidos* use the old mine for a hideout."

"Not likely," Slade replied. "Too close to town and the trail over there, which looks to be well-traveled. No, that isn't the answer, Felipe. Oh, the devil with it all! Let's head for home and something to eat and some shut-eye. I feel like the frazzled end of a misspent life."

After a long and weary trudge they reached the cabin. They attended to their hurts, grabbed off a snack washed down with hot coffee and dropped into bed, not to awaken till the shades of evening were drawing near.

While Felipe prepared a meal, Slade scrubbed the dye from his face and hands. Felipe regarded the change in his appearance and shook his head.

"How did they penetrate your disguise?" he wondered. "It seemed most perfect."

"My fingernails," Slade replied.

"The nails of the fingers?"

"That's right," Slade nodded. "I made a slip that came near to being fatal for both of us. I forgot to touch up my nails. They are a little different in coloring from those of a Mexican with a lot of Indian blood. Baker spotted them. I'm not sure he recognized me, but he figured something wasn't right and told Quijano. There was just the thickness of your knife blade between us and death, *amigo*."

Twelve

AFTER THE MEAL was eaten, Slade sat smoking and puzzling over those mule prints in the patch of soft ground below the old mine. He discarded Felipe's theory that the outlaws might hole up in the old mine. It was too close to town and the tunnel mouth was visible from the well-traveled trail running between Nuevo Laredo and Piedras Negras to the west. Any such activity in the neighborhood of the mine would almost certainly be noted and the authorities informed. Then the mine would become a death-trap for the bandits.

He toyed with the notion that perhaps the smuggled goods crossed the swollen river by boat and were transferred to the mules, but quickly discarded that also. In the first place, trying to ferry the river in time of high water was a hazardous undertaking under the best conditions. Secondly, boats could not be hidden, not here with patrols constantly riding both river banks.

He resolved to investigate the terrain in the vicinity of the mine and in the dark hour before dawn he rode out of Nuevo Laredo with that in mind.

"I'll go it alone this time," he told Felipe.

"Have care," cautioned the Mexican.

In the strengthening light of dawn he studied the terrain adjacent to the mine. To the south, beyond the trail, was thick chaparral growth with the purple crests of mountains looming in the distance. To the north the land was more open. He sent Shadow up the long rise that led to the river bank and for some minutes sat gazing across the turbulent flood. The ruins of the old Mission House showed stark and grim, the first rays of sunlight gilding the shattered walls. He estimated that the ruins rested on an elevation a little greater than the south bank of the river.

Slade rode the river bank for miles, and found nothing. He saw nobody save some wandering herdsmen with flocks of sheep and a few *vaqueros* from the greatest ranches farther to the south. Toward evening he turned and rode slowly back toward Nuevo Laredo. Nowhere could he find any evidence of a number of horses or a mule train passing either east or west. About three miles west of town he turned south to the main trail, the ground having become so broken and brush-grown as to be well nigh impassable. It seemed ridiculous to think that heavily laden animals could have possibly passed this way.

In the twilight he pulled to a halt on the crest of a long and gentle rise and sat gazing south toward the blue and bronze mountains shouldering the sky. Down there somewhere, rumor said, Sabida Quijano had his hidden stronghold, an almost inaccessible valley where he had built a village and caroused in feudal splendor with his hard-bitten outlaws, waited on by willing servitors who looked upon him as their benefactor. And with Quijano would be Cullen Baker taking part in the revels, making his plans and biding his time.

Where Quijano was, Baker would be.

However, Slade still believed that the solution of the mystery and the opportunity to kill or capture Cullen Baker lay somewhere in the stretch of country between Nuevo Laredo and the old mine.

He turned his gaze to the east and saw two horsemen bulge into view from behind a clump of thicket riding west, and riding fast, something like a mile and a half distant.

He glanced about, saw that there was enough brush flanking the trail to screen a horse and rider. He backed

Shadow into it far enough to conceal the horse and himself.

The two riders forged purposefully westward. Then, less than half a mile distant, they swerved from the trail and vanished into the brush that flanked the trail on the north.

To all appearances they were headed for the river bank. Why? Slade eased the black from the brush and sent him drifting down the opposite sag, keeping in the brush as much as possible.

It was now almost full dark but Slade had marked the spot where the two riders disappeared. It was a gap in the chaparral through which ran a faint game-trail. He pulled up beside the dark opening and sat peering and listening. No sound came from the thick gloom and no movement was apparent. He rode cautiously into the gap, holding the black to a slow walk, every sense vigilantly alert.

He sent Shadow ahead steadily until he knew the river bank must be less than two hundred yards distant, then pulled the big black to a halt. Ahead the ground conditions had changed. The brush still grew thick but had greatly lessened in height. A rider would loom above it, outlined against the sky.

Slade swung down from the saddle and stole forward on foot, Shadow pacing after him. He had covered but a few yards when he halted to listen. A second later his keen ears caught a sound ahead, a faint metallic jingle as of bridle irons clinking as a horse tossed its head. He froze to absolute stillness, laying his hand on Shadow's neck in warning. The big black stood perfectly motionless, his ears pricked forward; then he blew softly through his nose.

Slade's vigilance increased. The horse heard or saw something that was inaudible and invisible to him. For long minutes he stood listening, but the jingling was not repeated.

He stooped and cautiously groped over the ground until his fingers encountered a small rounded boulder. He worked it from its bed of earth, straightened up and with a quick, deft movement tossed it underhand into the darkness ahead. The stone hit the packed surface of the trail with a muffled thud.

The answer was instantaneous and startling. A crackling stutter of gunfire shivered the silence. Slade heard bullets clip off branches, spat against tree trunks, rip the ground. His hands streaked to his own guns but froze on the butts. From ahead came a prodigious crashing and the drum of hoofs on the trail, fading quickly toward the north.

For long minutes Slade stood motionless, listening. From over to one side and to the rear came the tiny jingle. Another moment and he was sure he heard a soft rustling on the opposite side of the trail and to the rear. The sound was repeated, this time a short distance ahead.

There was no doubt in Slade's mind that he had walked into a cleverly baited trap. Doubtless he had been spotted riding the river bank and the unseen watchers had reasoned that he would return to Nuevo Laredo and had laid their plans in accordance. The two riders from the east had been set to lure him into the chaparral and Slade angrily admitted to himself that he had fallen for the lure. Meanwhile their companions lay holed up in the brush, ready, when he came riding along through the lower growth.

And in all this Slade saw the cunning hand of Cullen Baker.

Again he heard a faint rustling in the brush. He was being surrounded. Any moment would come the rush, the blaze of guns. The attackers were behind and on both sides of him. His only line of retreat lay straight ahead. And ahead, not much more than a hundred yards distant, lay the insurmountable barrier of the river.

"Just the same, fellow, we've got to take it," he breathed into Shadow's ear. With a swift, smooth movement he swung into the saddle. His voice rang out, "Trail, Shadow! Trail!"

Instantly the great horse leaped forward. There was a chorus of yells, a wild banging of guns. Bullets whipped past Slade. Then they reached the river bank and stormed upward to its crest. Ten feet below rolled the yellow, frothing flood of the Rio Grande.

"Take it, Shadow! Take it!" Slade roared.

With a squeal of half anger, half terror, Shadow launched himself through the air and struck the water. Slade slipped from the saddle and gripped the horn as they went under. Down, down they went, the current pounding them. They rose slowly at first, then with a rush, and broke surface, to be instantly seized by the full force of the current.

Bullets spatted the water and ricocheted off but quickly they were whisked out of range and the firing ceased.

Desperately Slade fought to gain the bank, but the current steadily forced him away. Downstream they raced, Shadow snorting and blowing, swimming strongly. Slade clung desperately to the horn, swimming with his legs and his free arm.

His knowledge of geology told him that the limestone ledge would not be a perpendicular wall, it would be shelving and with a slope leading up to it. Close to the ledge the water should be shallow enough to give both him and the horse a foothold. The great danger was that the driving force of the current would sweep them over the ford and into the maelstrom of the down-river side, in which case they were doomed. Nothing could live amid the wild whirlpools and eddies.

Staring ahead, Slade could see the long line of phosphorescent glow that marked the ripple over the ford. It rushed toward him with appalling swiftness.

Another moment and they were in the seethe and whirl of frothing water pounding the rock, hurtling against the beetling wall.

It was the hard-packed cushion of deposited silt sloping upward to the crest of the ledge that saved them. As they struggled to get a footing, Shadow's irons and Slade's boots sank into the yielding surface. Floundering and clawing they strove to reach the surface of the ford.

Shadow made it first, scrambling upward over the broken stone and mud until he stood on the broad crest, snorting and blowing, the driving water coming less than halfway up his legs. Clinging to the bridle, Slade gained the dubious sanctuary.

He could never hope to wade across against the push of the current. After what seemed an eternity of exhausting effort he got his chest across the saddle and, writhing and squirming, forked the hull and felt the comforting support of the stirrups.

"Go to it, fellow!" he gasped.

Shadow began moving toward the south bank. Slade steeled himself. They had whipped the river, but there was a good chance that the patrol on the south bank might plug them full of holes. He listened intently for the harsh command to halt, which he was prepared to instantly obey.

He got a break. No challenge came from the darkness and a few minutes later the crossing was safely negotiated and he was circling the town.

He regained Felipe's cabin and after regaling the apprehensive Mexican with an account of his latest adventure, set himself to the dinner ready and waiting for him.

Thirteen

SLADE SAT for some time deep in thought. Finally he turned to the old man.

"Felipe," he said, "do you know the officer in charge of the *rurales* in this section?"

"*Si Capitan*, his office is here in Nuevo Laredo. He is a fine man."

"I want to see him and try and talk him into placing a patrol in the section around that old mine. And I have no authority down here, no authority to act against Quijano, Baker or anybody else."

"I will take you to the *capitan*," Felipe said. "Doubtless he will be at home now, smoking a *cigarro* after his evening repast. I know where he lives."

"That'll be fine," Slade answered. "Let's go."

Felipe was right. They found the captain at home. He invited them in courteously, but when his gaze fell upon Slade's tall form his eyes narrowed and his face hardened.

"I know you, *Señor*," he said coldly, in precise English. "You are El Halcon, the *bandido*, I believe. What do you in *Mejico*?"

"Yes, I've been called El Halcon," Slade admitted. "May have been called a bandit by some people, too, but that's never been proven."

"There are too many against whom such a charge has never been—proven," the captain said grimly. "We neither want nor need another."

Slade slipped something from the concealed secret pocket in his broad leather belt and handed it to the captain. The *rurale* stared at the famous silver star set on a silver circle, honored and respected by the law-abiding

104

on both sides of the Rio Grande—the badge of the Texas Rangers!

The captain swore, with feeling. "Now," he declared, "I will not suffer surprise if Sabida Quijano himself enters wearing on his breast a decoration of honor from *El Presidente!* El Halcon a Texas Ranger!"

"Well, you won't see Quijano come in, with or without the decoration," Slade told him. "In fact, I don't think you need worry any more about Quijano."

"What do you mean?" asked the captain.

"I mean," Slade predicted, "that most any day now you'll hear he is dead."

"That would indeed be a blessing," the captain declared.

"A mixed blessing," Slade replied.

"And what do you mean by that?"

"I mean that the man who is planning to kill him is also planning to take over his following. Then you'll know what real trouble is. You'll very shortly have a full-fledged revolution on your hands, and one that will very likely be successful, at least so far as northern Mexico is concerned."

The captain raised both fists over his head. "*Señor*, please do not speak in riddles," he begged. "Explain, please. But first sit down and smoke and be comfortable while we talk."

Slade accepted a chair and rolled a cigarette. He regarded the perturbed officer through the blue mist of the smoke.

"Ever hear of Cullen Baker?" he asked suddenly.

"Yes," the *rurale* returned. "About the worst outlaw your Texas ever spawned, which is saying considerable. But I understand he is dead."

"Well, he isn't," Slade answered. "He was right here in Nuevo Laredo a couple of nights back."

He briefly explained.

"And you're down here after Baker?"

"Yes," Slade replied. "I feel I am justified in acting against Baker in any manner that may offer, anywhere. But of course I have no authority to act against Quijano or his followers. That's why I've come to you. I'm playing a hunch that somewhere in the vicinity of that old mine is where the smugglers cross the river. Do you think that by any chance there is a ford somewhere around there that could be negotiated when the river is high as it is now?"

The captain's reply was similar to Felipe's. "I was born and brought up here and I never heard of such a thing," he declared positively. "It is inconceivable that such should exist and I not know about it."

Slade nodded gloomily. "But just the same they cross the river somehow," he said, "and I feel it's somewhere in that neighborhood. Would you station a patrol there for a few nights on the bare chance I'm right?"

"Yes, I will establish a patrol tonight, although I hardly think they will attempt a crossing no matter what method they employ, with the river raging as it is at present and with all indications that it will rise still more within the next few days."

"Maybe not," Slade admitted, "but there's a chance they might be moving some stuff they had cached somewhere. That might give you an opportunity to drop a loop on them. And I'd like to ride with that patrol."

"No reason why you shouldn't," said the captain. "In fact, I'll ride with it myself. There's a ten-thousand-pesos reward for Quijano, you know," he added with a smile.

"Sure hope you get a chance to collect it," Slade said.

The patrol was established shortly after dark. At Slade's suggestion the posse holed up in the brush just south of the trail, from which point they could see the crest of the river bank outlined against the stars.

"Nobody can come across there without us seeing

them," Slade pointed out. "The same goes for anybody riding the trail to the north."

The captain shook his head doubtfully. "I fear we are but wasting our time," he said. "The river is still rising. Well, we shall see."

The hours passed tediously. Midnight came and went, the great clock in the sky wheeled westward, and nothing happened. In the gray light of dawn they returned to town.

The following night the performance was repeated without variation. The captain grew more pessimistic.

"I fear you are wrong," he told Slade, "but we'll try it one more night at least."

Late that afternoon, Felipe, who had been scouting the town, entered the cabin hurriedly, his eyes big with excitement.

"*Capitan*," he said, "there is a whisper going the rounds of the *cantinas*, a whisper that says Sabida Quijano is dead. His horse fell off a cliff trail to the west and broke his neck!"

Fourteen

"So THE DEVIL put it over, and made it appear to be an accident," Slade commented. "He's smart, all right, and utterly ruthless. But he'll have to keep things moving if he wants to hold his bunch together and hang onto Quijano's following. He'll pull something soon, if he gets a chance, and he'll make the chance if we don't stop him pronto."

That night the stars shone dimly through a veil of haze. The high mist thickened as the night wore on, until the darkness was intense. The night was very still and the patrolmen holed up in the brush could hear the distant moan and mutter of the swollen river.

"Only an utter fool would attempt to cross that stream tonight," the captain declared. "*Señor,* we but waste our time."

"Looks sort of that way," Slade admitted.

The hours crawled past. The false dawn flitted ghost-like across the vast arch of the gloomy heavens. There came the deepening hush of the darkest hour before the real dawn.

"Yes, it looks like we've wasted another night," Slade remarked to the captain.

Suddenly Shadow blew softly through his nose. Slade tensed.

"My horse hears something," he breathed to the captain. He strained his own ears and a moment later caught a sound, a rhythmic clicking drawing steadily nearer from the north.

"Something coming," he breathed to the captain who

was trembling with eagerness. "Get set, they're close."

Nothing could be seen in the pitch dark, but the sound steadily loudened. Another moment and the advancing horses would reach the trail. He started to breathe a word of caution to the captain.

Before Slade could restrain him, the impulsive Latin acted—too soon. "Halt!" he bellowed in Spanish.

There was a jangling of bit irons and a popping of saddle leather in the dark ahead, then a blaze of gunfire. Bullets buzzed around the patrolmen who ducked and yelled and began banging off their guns at a great rate. Above the uproar sounded the beat of swift hoofs and a prodigious crashing as the outlaws took to the brush.

"After them!" howled the captain, driving his spurs home. After him pounded his men, yelling and shooting.

Slade took no part in the shooting, nor did he join in the futile pursuit. Hooking a leg over the saddle horn he waited for the patrol to return. Nearby a mule brayed, another snorted and snuffled. Slade rolled and lighted a cigarette. He knew the mules would not stray. He waited patiently till the patrol came straggling back, volleying curses. He called to them as they drew near and in another moment they were grouped around him.

"Well, we got the mules, anyhow," he told the captain. "Light up a couple of torches and let's see what we bagged."

The flare of the torches showed three of the long-eared creatures standing patiently beside the trail. The aparejos on their backs were bulged out.

The patrolmen rushed forward with exultant shouts. Then a sudden shrill-voiced malediction brought silence. One of the policemen was fingering the material of the aparejo he had started to rip open. He chattered excitedly in Spanish. His companions hurriedly drew back from the mules.

The packsack was soaking wet, and the mule that bore it dripped water, as did its two fellows!

Slade rode nearer. The captain turned toward him a face that looked sickly in the torchlight.

"I'm not superstitious," he said, "but that *does* look uncanny. They couldn't possibly have crossed that river."

"They're here," Slade pointed out.

"And with the look of animals that have been recently submerged," mumbled the officer, "but it is impossible!"

"Let's see what's in the packs."

The *rurales* seemed disinclined to touch the things so Slade opened one himself and spilled a shower of rifle parts and cartridges onto the ground. He glanced at the captain.

"This stuff undoubtedly came from north of the Rio Grande," he remarked. "A pity you didn't catch one of the hellions. You might have induced him to tell us something."

"If I ever lay hands on one he'll talk and be glad of the chance," the captain declared. "Do you think your *amigo* Cullen Baker was with them?"

"Wouldn't be surprised if he was convoying the bunch, from the swift way in which they acted," Slade replied. "I think he'll be present at any action, large or small, for a while. He knows he must strengthen his grip on the bunch, hold the late Quijano's following in line and consolidate his power."

"You mean Quijano is dead?" exclaimed the captain.

"So I understand," Slade answered. "Yes, Baker is the big skookum he-wolf now, and if he isn't stopped soon, well, you know what to expect."

"*Sangre de Cristo!*" exploded the *rurale.*

Slade chuckled. "You didn't do so bad tonight. A lot of *escopetas* and ammunition in those sacks."

"But the man we fear still ranges free and we know not how they cross the river," the captain replied.

"Well, we might as well gather up the loot and head for home," Slade suggested, glancing at the leaden sky wanly brightening with the dawn. "Looks like it might rain."

Fifteen

SLADE TURNED OUT to be a good weather prophet. The following night was a night of slashing rain and roaring wind. The captain glanced disgustedly at the streaming window.

"We're not going out tonight," he announced. "Nothing will be moving on such a night as this, and besides I prefer my men to have a little more time to get over their scare. They're not afraid of *bandidos*, except those that are in league with the Powers of Darkness, as they firmly believe this band is. They fear evil spirits more than bullets."

"I'll take the spirits," Slade said. He did not argue with the officer although he felt that he could very well be wrong. Neither wind nor rain would stop Cullen Baker if he had something in mind. He might even decide that it would be an excellent time for his operations, being familiar with the Mexican dislike of moving around in such weather.

Saying good night to the captain, Slade buttoned his slicker close and walked swiftly through the rain to Felipe's cabin. Felipe was dozing on one of the bunks and Slade didn't rouse him. He sat before the fire, smoking and thinking.

Patiently he went over every angle again and again and always the angles persisted in resolving into curves that eventually brought him right back to where he had started.

The laden mules had undoubtedly come from the north, and their soaked condition and that of their loads insisted that they had come through the waters of the river, which to all appearances was patently impossible. Slade began to wonder if Felipe might possibly have been right in his surmise that the outlaws had a hole-up in the old mine where perhaps the contraband had been stored and was moved out by degrees when opportunity offered. That could possibly explain the condition of the mules and the packs. The old working was undoubtedly a very wet one. Perhaps the goods had been stored and the mules corralled in some damp chamber where water dripped from the ceiling. Seemed highly unlikely though not altogether beyond the realm of reason. It appeared so near to an absurdity that Slade put it out of his mind, but it persisted in returning. Slade swore wearily and rolled another cigarette.

After a while Felipe roused up and made a pot of coffee. Slade noted that the rain was slackening, the wind losing much of its force. An hour before midnight the stars were peeping shyly through rifts in the clouds and only a gentle breeze was blowing.

Slade stood up, hitching his gun belts higher.

"Felipe," he said, "I'm going to have a look at that old mine. There's a possibility that you could be right and the *bandidos* might have a hole-up there."

"But, *Capitan*," Felipe protested, "if that really should be the case you will be going to almost certain death. I will go with you."

Slade shook his head. "No, I'd rather you stayed here," he said. "If I don't show up tomorrow, go to the captain and have him and his men search the mine. But don't worry, you'll see me tomorrow."

The truth of the matter was Slade felt Felipe had already stood enough. He didn't consider it fair to expose the old man to possible further danger.

"By the way," he said, "I see you have a bundle of torches in the corner there by the fireplace. I'll take a few of them with me. Might need a light."

He secured the torches and left the cabin. A few minutes later he had the rig on Shadow and was riding swiftly westward.

Some distance east of the mine Slade drew rein. He studied the starlit surroundings and then sent Shadow into the chaparral growth that flanked the trail on the south, and dismounted. He removed the bit from Shadow's mouth and loosened the cinches.

"You take it easy here till I come for you," he told the horse. "Plenty of grass and there's a trickle of water over there. Stay put, and don't go singing any songs to the stars. The less noise the better. Be seeing you!"

Slade approached the tunnel mouth. To all appearances it was deserted, but he paused, peering and listening, before entering the bore. He carefully groped his way along in the utter darkness. The black gloom remained undisturbed by sound or motion. He trailed the left wall with his hand and finally it encountered empty space. He had reached the point where the tunnel leading to the room in which he and Felipe had been imprisoned emptied into the main corridor.

Again he paused and heard nothing save the slow gurgle of water washing the opposite wall. He groped on for another hundred paces and then decided to light one of the torches.

The torch burned briskly, casting a ruddy glow over the beamed walls and ceiling. There was a constant drip of water from overhead. Shallow pools dimpled the uneven surface of the floor. Little streams trickled slowly in channels at the base of the side walls, for the corridor had a very slight but steady upward slope.

Slade noted that the wall and ceiling timbers cast back the torchlight in an iridescent bloom. They appeared to be covered with a glassy film. He peered at the smooth surface, touched it with a tentative finger, and with a geologist's knowledge understood the explanation of the phenomenon.

The dripping water was siliceous. During the course of untold years it had impregnated and coated the timbers until they were almost like petrified trees or stalactites. As such they would last forever. But the process, to reach its present state, must have taken a vast number of years. Yes, the mine was very old. Old, doubtless, when the Spaniard first set mailed foot on Mexican soil. Dug perhaps by the Aztecs, or even by the Toltecs, the people who inhabited Mexico before the Aztecs swarmed down from the north to take over their ancient empire.

Slade realized that the tunnel had been gradually changing course. At its mouth it trended to the west. Now, however, his plainsman's uncanny instinct for direction told him that it ran almost due north. He trudged on through the utter silence, broken only by the drip and gurgle of the water. To all appearances the ancient burrow had not been invaded for untold years.

And then abruptly he halted, his heart leaping exultantly in his breast. On the floor ahead was the indubitable evidence that a horse had passed this way and no great time before. Less than twenty-four hours, Slade judged.

For a moment he was tempted to put out the torch. Reassured by the continued silence and the sense of utter aloneness, he kept the torch burning and moved on. He had covered fully a mile when he halted abruptly.

Stretching from side to side of the tunnel was a wall of solid masonry, ponderous blocks two feet long by better than a foot in width, closely cemented together. He eyed the barrier with gloomy astonishment. To all appearances the blocks had been put in place many, many years before. He'd hit the end of the trail.

Sixteen

BUT WHY IN BLAZES, Slade wondered in bewilderment, would a horse or horses have been up the corridor if there was no egress! It didn't make sense.

He observed that shallow channels pierced the masonry at its base and against the side walls of the tunnel, through which water gurgled. Without a doubt there was a continuation of the corridor on that far side of the barrier.

Studying the wall he noted that the courses of the stone formed a pattern. Lines of jointure ran vertically from the floor to almost the roof of the tunnel and were intercepted, top to bottom, by horizontal lines, the whole constructing a rectangle five feet wide by perhaps seven in height. The intimation was that a door had once existed, now blocked with stone.

He approached the barrier and examined it closely. Suddenly his eyes fixed on something. The uniform color of the wall was dusty gray, but the edge of one of the blocks near the center showed yellowish. He traced the scar with his forefinger, rubbed it hard. The feel of it was quite different from the stone near the side wall. He slipped his knife from his pocket, opened it and drew the keen edge along the corner of the block. He uttered a sharp exclamation.

The knife edge had planed off a curling shaving!

The center blocks were not stone but wood, painted to simulate stone! He moved the knife point past the vertical line of jointure and scraped vigorously on a block near the tunnel wall. The steel rasped on stone. But a fresh attack on the center blocks brought off more shavings. The wood was porous and crumbly, very old. Not nearly so old as the supporting timbers, but it had undoubtedly been set in place many years before.

Slade slipped the knife back in his pocket. He felt over the surface of the barrier with eager fingers. Then he set his shoulder against the wooden blocks, a little off the center and shoved. Nothing happened. He moved to the other side of center and put forth more pressure. Slowly, the inner segment of the barrier began to move, and swung outward with a creaking of unoiled iron.

"A door!" Slade breathed.

It was a smooth piece of work. A casual prowler would decide that the tunnel had long since been walled up. Somebody was anxious to have the opening artfully concealed. Quijano's smugglers? Slade shook his head. An examination of the unpainted outer side of the door showed it old, rotten with damp decay. It had been in existence long before Sabida Quijano was born. Slade put forth his strength and swung the door wide open. As he stepped through the opening, the door swung back to fit smoothly with the stone jambs.

Slade noted that a tarnished metal handle was fastened to the wood so that from the side on which he now stood the door could be opened without difficulty. He held his torch aloft and peered forward. The tunnel ran as before, only now it slanted steeply downward. After lighting a fresh torch from the stump of the one he held, he set out again.

For a good two hundred yards the steep slant continued, then the rock floor abruptly leveled off. Here the shoring timbers were replaced by columns of stone that supported the cracked and fissured roof of the bore.

The tunnel was much wetter. The water no longer trickled, it streamed. As Slade continued, the streams became spouts that drove downward with considerable force. He was drenched from head to foot and forced to shield the torch to prevent it sputtering out. Gradually he became conscious of a vast murmuring and rustling that quivered the air and vibrated the rock walls.

At first he was at a loss to account for the strange sound. Then he understood and stopped dead, his flesh crawling. The eerie noise was made by swiftly running water, a vast flood of water rolling irresistibly to mingle with the Gulf of Mexico. He was beneath the mighty torrent of the Rio Grande!

Slade glared upward at the cracked and broken stone roof, through which streamed and spouted the icy water. His hair prickled on his scalp, his skin felt clammy and cold as he started to walk again. It was weird, trudging through the black dark relieved only by the flicker of his torch, with the stupendous volume of the swollen Rio Grande boiling over his head. He tried to reassure himself that the cracked roof had withstood the crushing weight for ages and would doubtless withstand it for ages yet to come. But the probability was cold comfort against what his lively imagination told him would happen should the river burst through.

Despite his apprehensions, he slowed his pace, motivated by an intense curiosity that for the moment displaced all else. The flat spaces between the stone pillars were sculptured with strange carvings that showed considerable, if crude, artistic merit.

They were old, unbelievably old. Slade was familiar with Aztec and Toltec carvings. These were neither. They were older than the Aztec and even the Toltec cultures. He realized he was looking upon the work of a people who must have inhabited the land before the Toltec invasion, perhaps antedating even the people the Toltecs found when they migrated to what was now Mexico.

He gazed at the carvings, fascinated by this wan glow from the darkness of Time's night. He noted that some of the supporting pillars were sculptured in bas-relief. There were hunting scenes, many of them, portrayals of men wrestling—short, powerful men with lank black hair and slanted eyes, but with skins apparently scarcely darker than his own. There were depictions of other sports and a few battle scenes. One, which was very beautiful, featured a charge of troops armed with spears, shields and short swords, with a convoy of prisoners being marched off in the distance.

A peaceful people, these long gone primitives, Slade decided, judging from the many portrayals of everyday happenings and the few of warlike activities. Who were they, these people of the world's dawn? And why had they dug this ancient tunnel under the river? To afford a passage for treasure from the north? Possibly. Slade felt, however, that it more likely had military significance and was perhaps part of the outer line of defense of the people who built it. The Rio Grande had always been a boundary. It was the line between the Aztecs and the savage tribes of the northern plains and mountains. That much history knew. Doubtless the Aztecs had to storm the river when they swept down on the Toltecs, and it was quite probable the Toltecs found it the outpost of the people they conquered when *they* forged down from the north.

Slade was so intrigued by the strange place in which he found himself that he forgot the almost incessant deluge of water that drenched his clothes and set a clammy cold eating into his very bones. He forgot even the eerie rustling and moaning of the river gnawing away at the stones over his head. He was consumed by curiosity and thrilled by the knowledge that the seemingly unexplainable crossing of the river by the smugglers was no longer a mystery. This was the way by which they outwitted pursuit. No wonder the mules and the packsacks were drenched as if they had swum the waters of the Rio Grande. His torch burned low and he had but one remaining. Still he lingered, engrossed by that which any archaeologist would have given his eyeteeth to view.

He was brought back from the dead past by a sound that was not of the dripping water or the moaning river, a sound that came from the darkness behind him. He whirled about, caught a glimpse of a number of lights bobbing toward him from the ancient mine. He heard a startled shout, then a roaring, bellowing voice that he instantly recognized as belonging to Cullen Baker.

"Shoot the Texas Ranger!" howled Baker. "Kill him! Kill him!"

The tunnel rocked and pounded to the boom of shots cramped between the rocky walls. A bullet whined past, struck a pillar and showered the wet floor with stone chips. Slade threw the torch to the floor and raced along the water-streaming tunnel. Behind him sounded yells and the pounding of booted feet. More guns boomed, the reports came thunderous, hollow. The rock walls seemed to reel and sway under the terrific vibrations set up by the explosions in the restricted space. Lead buzzed around him like a swarm of disturbed bees. He jerked his own guns, whirled and sent a volley storming through the darkness to add to the uproar.

Shouts and a scream of pain rose amid the crashing reports. Evidently one or more of his shots had found a mark and the pursuers were momentarily thrown into confusion. Slade ran as he had never run before.

But the pursuit came on. Again and again their guns bellowed, but it was blind shooting and Slade, hugging the rock wall, was untouched so far. The tunnel was beginning to slant gently upward now and the streaming water was less of deluge proportions.

There *must* be a way out of this infernal badger burrow! There must! The thought pounded through his brain. But if it was going to do him any good, he'd have to reach it soon. He winced as bullets knocked chips from the stone close to his face. His ears rang. The magnified vibratory impulses seemed to detach the flesh from his bones. A slug grazed his cheek. Another ripped the soaked sleeve of his shirt.

"They can't keep missing!" he panted. "I'm bound to stop one sooner or later. I— *God Almighty!*"

The two words that burst from his writhen lips were not profane ejaculation. They were a prayer! In the flame-splashed darkness behind him had sounded a crash like the splintering of worlds, followed instantly by a roaring and rushing as if all the stored-up rains of the heavens were loosed upon the drowned earth.

The incessant vibrations set up by the shooting had brought down a section of the roof. The Rio Grande, triumphant after ages of frustration, was pouring its flood into the tunnel.

Seventeen

GASPING, PANTING, Slade fled wildly up the gently sloping bore, while behind him thundered the unchained waters of the Great River. One thought pounded in his numbed brain—to find an exit from this terror. Gone was all thought of his pursuers, they were doubtless crushed and strangled under the fallen roof. And for once in his life, El Halcon knew fear—the blind and awful fear born of the loosed and raging powers of Nature, against which no human strength or courage could suffice. Only one of unsound mind would not have known terror at such a moment. All that was left to him was flight, mad, unreasoning flight spurred by the wild, cold thrill of terror.

Over the cracked and broken floor he reeled and stumbled, with the mighty thunder ever louder in his ears. The slope of the tunnel was steeper now, a steady upward trend.

He fumbled a match from its waterproof container as he ran and after several futile attempts managed to scratch it against the barrel of his gun and touch it to the head of his last oil-soaked torch. The torch sputtered, flickered, flared up and burned brightly.

Up and up the long slope, gasping, panting, dizzy with fatigue, Slade fled. He dared not slacken his pace although the pounding of his overworked heart threatened to burst his chest and his laboring lungs seemed a flame of searing fire.

Then with startling abruptness the tunnel ended, ended at a flight of six or seven worn stone steps stretching upward to what appeared to be the unbroken roof. As Slade staggered up the steps he saw that which brought hope surging back through the clammy blanket of despair. The roof directly over the narrow landing above the topmost step was not of stone but of ancient unpainted wood. He crashed his shoulders against the barrier. It splintered, flew upward and out with a screech of turning hinges. Slade scrambled through the opening and staggered away from its black mouth, dimly aware that his boots rang on dry stone and that about him, uprearing in a flood of silvery moonlight, were cracked, broken and unroofed stone walls.

He turned at a sound.

From the tunnel mouth rushed, not a flood of tawny water, but Cullen Baker, his features contorted with terror and hate.

Slade's nerves instantly hardened. His hands flashed to his guns as flame gushed toward him. He reeled back from the shock of a bullet slitting the flesh of his upper arm. Then his own Colts boomed.

For the third and last time, Cullen Baker and El Halcon shot it out. As the hammers of Slade's guns clicked on empty shells, Baker staggered back. He tried to lift the gun he held, but it sagged in his nerveless hand. Back and back he reeled toward the black opening in the floor, and even as a froth of yellow water gushed upward he fell, fell into the muddy flood that instantly receded, bearing the outlaw's body on its crest.

With the jerky movements of an automaton Slade holstered his empty guns. He stared dully at the black opening into which Cullen Baker had vanished.

"Guess that's one river he won't swim out of," he muttered. He turned and reeled blindly through a rent in the shattered wall and out into the still, white flood of moonlight.

His strength left him and he sank to the ground, to all

appearances as dead as Cullen Baker in his watery grave.

When he finally roused, the moon was much lower in the sky and the east was paling with the dawn. Beside him were the broken walls of the old Mission House into which the tunnel emptied. In the distance were a few pinpoints of light.

"Must be Laredo," he mumbled, regarding them owlishly. One corner of his brain insisted that he had business in Laredo. But still gripped by the nightmare of his experience, his numbed mind regarded the matter with indifference. However, with a resigned sigh he got painfully to his feet and stumbled toward those distant sparkles.

As he trudged on through the morning, his strength returned somewhat and his brain cleared of cobwebs and when he finally reached the town he was back to something like normal. He paused at a small eating house for some badly needed food and coffee. The sleepy waiter who served him glanced curiously at his drenched clothes but was apparently too drowsy to ask questions.

After eating, Slade secured tobacco and papers and enjoyed a smoke. Feeling much better, he hunted up a livery stable, hired a horse and after attending to the slight bullet cut in his arm, he headed back to Mexico to retrieve Shadow.

He paused long enough to rouse the customs official. "Take a troop over to the ruins of the old Mission House and hole up there," he directed after a brief summary of what had occurred. "I think some time today or tonight you'll have a chance to bag a few small-fry smugglers. I don't think you'll have any trouble with them. I've a notion they're just some of Quijano's dupes. Be seeing you."

With the star of the rangers pinned on his breast Slade had no difficulty crossing the bridge. As he rode west he wondered if enough water was pouring from the tunnel mouth to inundate the lowlands south of the mine. But when he reached the terrain there was no sign of flood. He transferred to Shadow and rode up the slope to the tunnel mouth.

Water was trickling from it, but not much. Evidently the fallen roof had completely blocked the passage. Soon silt from the flood waters would fill the bore and it would be as if it never was. He turned Shadow and rode back to Nuevo Laredo and Felipe's cabin. He was near complete exhaustion and after giving Felipe a terse account of what had happened, he fell into bed and slept until evening.

"And I suppose you will be riding north again, *Capitan?*" Felipe observed as they smoked by the fire.

"Yes, Captain McNelty will have something lined up for me when I get back to the Post, the chances are," Slade replied. "I want you to see the *rurale* captain and tell him Cullen Baker is dead, that he died on Texas soil, and that the Rio Grande took care of all or most of his bunch. With no leader left alive, his following that was Quijano's will quickly dissipate. The captain can go back to chasing sheep thieves. No, I don't want to see him. The yarn sounds so incredible, I'm afraid he'd think I'm either loco or lying."

But when Slade later regaled Captain Jim McNelty with an account of his experiences, the old ranger commander tugged his mustache and looked thoughtful.

"I've heard a legend dealing with that old tunnel, a legend that's existed along the Rio Grande for many years, although it was supposed to be situated farther east, around Brownsville. I recall reading a magazine article once, relating a story supposed to have been told the writer by an old Indian who had seen the tunnel when he was a small boy but couldn't remember just where it was located. I put it down as just another yarn, but it would appear there was something to it. All sorts of stories like that kicking around in this corner of the world where anything can happen and usually does. I wonder who dug the darn thing in the first place?"

"It was old, mighty old, excavated heaven knows when," Slade said. "I've a notion the old Mission Fathers discovered it when they built their Mission House. Doubtless they recognized its value in a troubled country as an escape route across the river if they were attacked by hostile tribes, as many of those posts were. I'd say they set those doors in place, artfully painted to simulate stone. Somehow, Quijano stumbled onto it, and he in turn recognized its value as an aid in his smuggling operations. It sure worked for him, all right, and sure had everybody puzzled. No wonder those mules had the appearance of having swum the Rio Grande at a time when everybody conceded the impossibility of swimming it.

"Yes, it was an old construction, strange. An archaeologist would have gone plain loco with delight had he gotten a look at it. None ever will, however. The river has taken it back for keeps."

"Yes, and the Rio Grande knows how to guard her secrets," said Captain Jim. "And her dead," he added. "Well, it all ended proper and I've got another little chore ready for you, if you feel up to it."

"After Cullen Baker, I feel up to anything," Slade grinned. "Let's go!"

The End

Bradford Scott was a pseudonym for **Leslie Scott** who was born in Lewisburg, West Virginia. During the Great War, he joined the French Foreign Legion and spent four years in the trenches. In the 1920s he worked as a mining engineer and bridge builder in the western American states and in China before settling in New York. A bar-room discussion in 1934 with Leo Margulies, who was managing editor for Standard Magazines, prompted Scott to try writing fiction. He went on to create two of the most notable series characters in Western pulp magazines. In 1936, Standard Magazines launched, and in *Texas Rangers*, Scott under the house name of **Jackson Cole** created Jim Hatfield, Texas Ranger, a character whose popularity was so great with readers that this magazine featuring his adventures lasted until 1958. When others eventually began contributing Jim Hatfield stories, Scott created another Texas Ranger hero, Walt Slade, better known as *El Halcon*, the Hawk, whose exploits were regularly featured in *Thrilling Western*. In the 1950s Scott moved quickly into writing book-length adventures about both Jim Hatfield and Walt Slade in long series of original paperback Westerns. At the same time, however, Scott was also doing some of his best work in hardcover Westerns published by Arcadia House; thoughtful, well-constructed stories, with engaging characters and authentic settings and situations. Among the best of these, surely, are *Silver City* (1953), *Longhorn Empire* (1954), *The Trail Builders* (1956), and *Blood on the Rio Grande* (1959). In these hardcover Westerns, many of which have never been reprinted, Scott proved himself highly capable of writing traditional Western stories with characters who have sufficient depth to change in the course of the narrative and with a degree of authenticity and historical accuracy absent from many of his series stories.